# IVY & TY

*Love Wasn't Meant For A Dope Boy*

## BREANNA RENEE

# Ivy Marie Richardson

"Ma, can you please watch Kacey for me tonight? I don't ask you for much," I said, damn near on bended knee as we stood on the front porch of the home we shared together. Tonight was Tuesday, and she knew I had to go in at the club.

Between her and my child's father not wanting to keep my son, I was either late or had to call in. I wasn't trying to do either of the two, mainly because I was on a mission to live the way I wanted to. My lifestyle wasn't cheap, which meant I had to secure the bag. My goal was to stack as much as I could so me and my son, Kacey, would be able to have our own spot.

Right now, it was me, my son, my mother, and my grandpa under one roof. The house may have been spacious, but my mother's vibe could haunt you from a distance. She didn't want me here, and it was no secret. Never did she make me feel welcomed here, even if I paid the bills and put food in the house. She'd rather criticize my parenting or my job.

Thankfully, it wasn't her housed to make the decisions to throw me out. It was her parents', and since my grandma died a few years back, my grandpa had the final say-so. He loved me enough to open his doors for me and my child once I broke it off with my baby's daddy. Yes, I could've went and got my own place right away after the breakup, but I had my reasons. I just wouldn't get into that right then.

"Why don't you ask that no-good bastard to watch his fucking son? What you call 'work' is far from a real job. I didn't have this child, so I shouldn't have to watch him." She rolled her eyes and took a puff from her cigarette.

I hated the smell of those things with a passion, but they helped her cope most of the time. That or the bottle. My mother was truly fucked up in the head. Everything from the past destroyed her mental. That was why she could never move on. That was why she could never love me like a mother should.

I sighed and sucked my teeth. "You know that was my first option, but he's busy—"

"Busy doing what, Ivy? Hell, you would've been better off staying with his ass. At least when y'all were together, he didn't mind keeping his son, but you let a little cheating run you off." She laughed. "These women nowadays. You know you can't make it without that man. Might as well go back to sleeping with him, and then maybe he'll watch his child for a good hour or two," she spat.

I couldn't even get offended if I tried. I was used to her words when it came to me, and still, I always kept it respectful toward her. She would never change.

"Wow, are you serious? So I'm supposed to stay with

a nigga who doesn't treat me the way I deserve to be treated? Ma, please. I'm not doing this with you tonight," I said, starting to get irritated by the minute. The only reason I even asked her to watch Kacey was because his father, Rashad, was in his feelings. He seen a picture of me from the club with a guy and assumed I had to be fucking him when I wasn't. I tried to explain to him it was just promotional photos for the club, but of course, he'd rather curse me out than to believe me. Typical shit.

Rashad was the petty type. If I pissed him off, then he wouldn't get Kacey. If I didn't want to fuck with him, then he wouldn't give me any money. It was the type of shit like that that let me know, for a fact, leaving him was the best thing to do, not just for me, but for Kacey as well. A nigga wasn't about to control me or my life just because he felt like he could. It just wasn't right. I felt as if though Rashad should have the decency to work with me rather than against me simply because I was Kacey's mom. I guess I was wrong because all he wanted to do was argue me down and try to make me feel guilty for the shit he put me through.

I couldn't lie and say I didn't miss him. It'd only been six months, and even still, sometimes in the beginning, I would double back to him, but this time, I was serious. I had to get my shit together, fast. Although I was only twenty-three, I had major responsibilities.

"Oh, now you got some worth? Child, please." She laughed and shook her head. "You not fooling nobody, Ivy. Call. His. Daddy." She broke it down. "I'm done raising kids." She blew the smoke in my face before she put her cigarette out.

"You didn't even raise me!" I shouted while the tears fell from my eyes, and she walked off. The slamming of the front door made my heart jump outside of my chest. "Fuck." I covered my mouth in distress. If I had the time, I would break down right on my grandparents' porch.

Looking at the time on my phone, I knew I had to think of something quick. If I spent another minute here, I would be late. I sighed and quickly got myself together because if my son saw me like this, he would start to ask questions that I didn't have the answers to.

Kacey was three going on thirteen. He knew so many things, things that I wouldn't expect for him to know.

"Mommy, is Grandma gonna watch me?" he said as I got into my all-white AMG Mercedes-Benz. Rashad bought it for me for my twenty-first birthday, and I knew the only reason he let me keep it was because of Kacey. He knew I had to get him from A to Z.

"No, Kacey, not tonight," I said, keeping it brief.

"You're going to spend the night with daddy," I said, quickly thinking of something.

"I am?" he asked excitedly. Kacey loved his father just like he loved spending time with him. I didn't mind it though, because everything he had at his dad's best believe he had it with me. Our child was spoiled. I could admit that, but I also poured and instilled love in my child. I refused to be the kind of mother mine was.

I didn't bother to call Rashad and let him know we were coming over. I was sure he'd be home and he wouldn't dare act crazy in front of his son. I wasn't fucking with him, but Kacey was his son, and he was free. Why shouldn't he watch him while I went to work?

"Yes."

"I love it at Daddy's. Are you coming too?" he asked me while I started up the car and proceeded to drive off.

"Not tonight, baby. I have to work."

"Work?" he said in a funny tone.

"That's what I said."

"Grandma Joy said what you do isn't work. It's a cry for help," he said while I gasped.

"She said that to you?" I was almost in disbelief. I knew my mother wasn't a fan of me or the fact that I was a bottle girl at the club, but was she really that heartless that she'd bad-mouth me in front of my own son? Her own grandson? A damn shame.

"Yeah and some other things," he said, putting his head down.

I pulled over to the side of the road and looked back at him. "Kacey, you know mommy loves you with everything inside of her right?" I said, and he nodded his head. "You know there's nothing I won't do for you? Everything I do is for you. You're my everything. Never let anyone make you feel like I don't care or I'm doing something wrong. I would never. I love you, son, always."

"I know, Mommy. You a real one. I love you too," he said while I laughed a little and then smiled.

"My big boy." I blew him a kiss and then continued to drive to Rashad's. He stayed about forty minutes away from us, and that was the main reason why he got Kacey's on the weekends. Neither of us wanted to drive the long distance every day.

Rashad was a "get money" nigga who was born into money, so he damn sure wasn't staying just anywhere. No, he had a nice penthouse in uptown Miami with the perfect view. Sometimes I missed it, and sometimes I missed him, but all the time I was tired.

When we arrived at Rashad's house, Kacey was damn

near knocked out. Meanwhile, the whole car ride over here, I spent my time manifesting a better situation. I didn't want to be a failure as a woman or a mother. I knew what Kacey saw when he looked at me, but I couldn't say the same when I looked in the mirror at myself.

Getting out of the car, I grabbed Kacey's book bag and tablet for him. "Come on, baby. We're here," I said, waking him all the way up.

He jumped out the car so fast once he realized we were at his dad's, leaving me behind.

I could hear him knocking at the door from a distance, but there was no answer. I still had my key and was about to use it until Rashad finally came to the door dressed in nothing but some basketball shorts. I could tell he'd just woke up.

"Daddy!" Kacey yelled excitedly.

Rashad shot me a confusing look that only lasted for a good three seconds because he was loving on his son. "What's up, son? You missed your daddy?" he asked, picking him up from the ground while he kissed his forehead a few times.

"Yes." Kacey laughed while I stood there with my arms crossed.

"You gon' let us in or what?" As much as this was beautiful thing to watch. I had to be at work soon. I was pushing it by the minute.

Rashad said nothing. Instead, he opened his door wider for me to enter it. I was a woman, with trust issues, so I looked around his place. The first place my eyes shifted to was the living room. It wasn't as clean as it usually was when I was here. There were blankets, pillows, and two glasses on the wooden table. I could only wonder who he had over here. I honestly didn't know if he was bringing bitches over here or not, but I didn't play that shit when it came to Kacey. There would be no other woman in my child's face, trying to play mommy because he only had one—me.

"Daddy, I can go play my game?" Kacey asked while I shifted my attention back to them.

"Yeah, do you. Everything still set up for you in your room," he said, and Kacey was about to run off.

"Wait, no hugs and kisses for your mom?" I said, making him stop in his tracks.

"Bye, Mommy. I love you," he said, giving me a hug while I smiled and hugged him back. His hugs were the best. They gave me hope and joy at the same time.

"I love you more." I kissed his lips, and then he successfully ran off.

"My phone off or something? 'Cause last time I checked, my shit was working perfectly," Rashad said while I rolled my eyes.

"I gotta work tonight. My mama's trippin', and you're his father," I said, taking a seat at the island.

"I am. Still, you could've called first."

I could've sat here and argued him down. I could've gone on about him possibly not answering or purposely ignoring me because he was still mad about those photos, but instead, I took the high road. "Okay, Rashad. I'll call next time," I simply stated, about to get up until he came and stood in front of me.

"You miss me?"

"Sometimes," I admitted.

"Well, I miss you all the time, Ivy. What you doing? Come back to the crib. You know you want to. All that dealing with yo' mama driving you crazy. It's all over your face. Over here, you don't gotta deal with none of that." He was somewhat right. Who wouldn't miss this luxurious lifestyle and the beautiful view it came with? Still, I deserved better. What I longed for, Rashad couldn't give me, and that was loyalty.

"Just because you miss me doesn't mean you'll respect me, Rashad. We're better off just co-parenting, and you know that."

"I don't. You still love me, and I'm gon' always love you. You really wanna start over with somebody new?" he said while I shook my head.

"Starting over with another nigga is the last thing on my mind. I'm not even fully over you. The only thing I'm interested in doing is being a great mother to Kacey."

"And you can't do that shit if you working at bullshit ass clubs. How the fuck you think that makes me feel when niggas come back and tell me my baby mama showing her ass for tips? You that low, shorty?" He said while I frowned.

"It was alright when you met me at a club though, right? I was doing the same thing. It's just when we got together, I stopped."

I wasn't new to the club scene. I was a bottle girl for a few years before, but once Rashad came along, he made me quit my job. The pay was good, so I went back after the breakup, just to a different club. I wasn't planning on working there for forever. I just needed to save up for maybe a year give or take, and then I'd be out. I knew the club hustle. Trust. That's why I was making more money than a lot of girls in the same position as me.

"So why yo' ass go back then? I can still provide for you and my son both."

"Because, Rashad, your money comes with limits, and I don't need it," I stated. The only reason he downplayed what I said is because he knew I was right. He could continue to provide for Kacey, and I'd be good. "I don't give a fuck what anybody has to say. I'm not a stripper, I'm not fucking for money, and I'm not doing anything wrong. I'm a bottle girl, nothing more, nothing less. I don't even feed into that lifestyle. I make my money and go home."

"You know what? I don't believe shit you say, Ivy."

"That's fine because I'm not your bitch, and I don't have to report to you," I said, attempting to get up from my seat, but he wouldn't allow it.

"You gon' always be my bitch," he said, placing his hand on my thigh while he started to caress it gently.

His touch had an effect on me, and it probably would always. But in my mind, I thought the more days passed by, the stronger I'd be when it came to not fucking with him. I was trying, but I wasn't perfect. That baby mama and baby daddy hold was something serious, okay? If you knew, you knew. However, so far so good.

Grabbing his hand before it went any further up my thigh, I spoke, "Make sure Kacey is on time for school tomorrow. I can pick him up afterwards."

"That's all you gotta say to me?" he said, moving closer to my face.

Was it bad that I wanted to kiss him? I almost did until Kacey came running down the stairs.

13

"Come on, Daddy! Let's go play Mario Brothers. I'ma bust yo' butt."

Rashad looked over to Kacey but never left from my presence. "I'm coming, Kacey, but you know yo' dad want all the smoke."

"Come on then." Kacey laughed while he ran back up the stairs.

"One game with you, and then it's bedtime, Rashad. I'm serious. He already has a hard time waking up in the morning," I said, pushing him out the way so that I could get up from my seat.

"Man, I got this, but if you're so worried about my daddy skills, how about you come back over here when you get off."

I saw right through him. He wanted me to come back to his place for one reason and one reason only—to have sex.

"My bed works for me just fine," I said, headed to the front door. I made a promise to myself that I would no longer run back to Rashad unless it was something solid. I wasn't just a jump-off I was the type of woman who deserved commitment.

"Ivy?" he called my name.

"Yes?" I said, turning on my heels.

"You know yo' time at the club is limited right? I let

you make it, but now my patience is running real thin," he said, and I sighed.

"Good night, Rashad."

*

"About time you made it, miss mamas. I thought I was gonna have to feed Montell some more lame ass excuses for you. You know I can't lie for shit. Apparently, you got six dogs, and they all seem to be dying within the last six months," Cassidy said as she applied some mascara to her already-full lashes.

"Thanks. Tonight has been hard. Between my mother and Rashad, I don't know how long I'm gonna be able to even work here," I ranted.

"Rule number forty-four, never let no nigga or no bitch get in the way of your paper. You know this," she said, starting to run through her hair with the curling iron.

"Easy for you to say."

"Yo, Cassidy, you up next, ma," Darren, the security guard, announced.

"Sure thing. Just give me a minute," she said while she sighed and looked down at me as I sat at her station. "Well... talk, Ivy. I don't got all day," she said, crossing her arms.

I hesitated to even say a word to her, even though I knew she had my back and didn't mind the conversation. She was my only true friend at the club, and even though the strippers, the bottle girls, and bartenders all seemed liked they had it out for each other, Cassidy had me.

She took me under her wing as soon as I got here a few months ago, and for that, I would always respect her.

"I just feel like I'm not doing enough. It's like nothing I do is good enough. People always have something to say, and it's like I gotta be strong for Kacey. I can't fail him, but a part of me feels that I've already have," I said with watery eyes.

Cassidy smacked her lips and sighed. "Come with me," she said, more so telling than asking me. She grabbed my hand and pulled me into a bathroom that was near. "Ivy, get your shit together. Nobody in this world owes you a damn thing. The sooner you learn this, the better."

"I'm trying, Cas," I cried while she tilted her head and puckered her lips.

"No you're not. Look, it's not about you. You said it yourself you're doing this for Kacey. Once you enter that parking lot out there, your feelings disappear like a thief in a night. Baby, you gotta be tough in a skirt around here. The minute these bitches see you sweat is when they decide to pick you off. Stay solid and chase that bag, baby girl. You got this," she said, touching my chin.

I sighed and wiped my tears. "You're right."

"Always. Never have I steered you wrong. That's why, when I say this, I want you to listen loud and clear. Let Rashad's ass go. That's the only way you gon' see yo' full potential."

"What if I can't?" I mumbled.

"Tuh, you can, and you will. I'm not the type to judge. If you wanna go back to him, do that. But I also won't stop myself from applauding you when you move the fuck around from him either. Kacey first, the bag second. You hear?"

I nodded.

"Good. Clean that face. Your shift already started," she said, turning away to leave.

"Cas… thank you, really," I told her while she just smiled and then walked away.

"Bitch, I know you didn't sit yo' silicone ass in my chair. You better raise up," I heard Cassidy yell, and I laughed some. Cassidy was that bitch around here, and everyone knew it. She didn't let anybody see her sweat, nor did she tolerate any disrespect. Not only that, but she was the breadwinner around here, bringing in ten times more than any other stripper. Everybody who came here wanted to see Cassidy shake some ass. She was damn good at her job, which made the other girls envious of her.

After I got myself together, I went back into the

dressing room to get dressed.

"Ivy, Montell wants to see you in his office right now," Darren said, popping up once again. "Here I come," I said, running the flat iron through my twenty-eight inches of Brazilian straight bundles. No matter how bad I felt, I made sure I looked damn good on the job. Niggas wasn't tipping a bitch that wasn't bad. Cassidy taught me that.

I applied some lip gloss and then followed Darren out. He led me to Montell's office, and from outside the door, I could hear loud moans. Daren knocked three times and then stepped back.

"Who is it?" Montell asked while I heard a loud commotion.

"It's me, boss. I got Ivy out here, like you asked me too," Darren said.

I cringed at the fact that I had to go in there after he'd just got done fucking one of these dirty ass bitches. Besides, I was sure I knew what he was going to say to me. Something about me being late.

"Give me five minutes," he said.

I was about to walk away until Darren grabbed my arm gently. "Boss man said five minutes, so you wait five minutes, pretty," he said while I sighed and nodded. I had no damn choice but to wait.

Ten minutes later, out walked Montell and one of the strippers named Aqua. It wasn't my business, but Montell was known to fuck plenty of females who worked here. Some fucked for a higher pay, some fucked for longer stage time, and some just fucked because they had something to prove. I couldn't relate.

Montell whispered something into Aqua's ear, and then she threw me a smirk and walked away. "Come take a walk with me," Montell said while I followed his lead.

I always got creepy ass vibes from him, but he never tried anything with me. I just didn't understand what was so appealing about fucking a nigga who was pushing fifty.

"You think I didn't realize you strolling up in here fifteen minutes late? I know everything around here. This here is my club."

*So this is what the conversation was about? Not surprised at all.* "Sorry, Montell. Something came up. It won't—"

"Rule 29?" He cut me off and questioned me.

"Never apologize for anything," I stated, and he nodded.

"Exactly. I'ma tell you this one time and one time only, little miss Ivy. If you're late again, then yo' ass is out. Too many times I done let you slide. I don't care if you are a favorite here. These bitches see you getting away with shit and start thinking it's okay. I can't have that. Understood?" he said, lighting his cigar.

"Yeah, Montell," I replied while he blew smoke from his mouth and nose.

"Good. You working floor three tonight," he said, about to walk off until I grabbed his arm. "Floor three? Why? I never work floor three," I said, completely shook while he looked down at my grip and then back at me. I quickly let him go and stepped back some.

"Don't question me. Yo' light-bright ass gone work whichever floor I tell you to. Now go get changed into something else. You not showing enough ass or breasts for my liking. Them niggas upstairs got the money to see both. Don't play with my damn money, Ivy." He pointed his finger in my face and began to walk off. "Oh yeah," he said, stopping in his tracks. "You working until closing tonight too," he said, and I tried to remain calm. Montell was acting like such an asshole today—shit, that was every day really.

"Yeah, okay, Montell," I said, walking right back into the dressing room to change.

The whole time I was in there, I started to feel slightly nervous. I was confident as hell, mainly because I knew I was fine. I had a nice frame, full lips, and the perfect amount of ass. My boobs sat up just right because after I had Kacey, I got a reduction and a lift. All of those things, men noticed, but I got the most compliments on my face. I was told that I was beautiful at least a hundred times a night.

After I got dressed, I took the elevator to the third floor. I made it just in time to see my girl Cassidy go on stage.

"Alright, ladies and gentlemen, welcome to Club Wishes. I need y'all to pull out those big dollar bills for my girl Cassidy. Not no chump change. Y'all niggas needa let it rain, let it rain. This ass here is exclusive, you hear?" DJ Dolla yelled while "Big Booty" by Gucci Mane and Megan Thee Stallion played out loud. As soon as Cassidy touched that stage, the crowd went crazy, and the dollar bills went flying.

Watching her out there was mesmerizing. I could only imagine how the niggas felt. My girl was talented on that pole here at Club Wishes.

Montell called it that because he said at this establishment, every wish anyone made before stepping foot into this mothafucka would come true by the end of the night. He wasn't lying. For the right price, these girls would do anything. I saw it with my own eyes.

"Ivy," Marissa, one of the bottle girls, said, getting my attention. "I know you working here on floor three tonight. Wanna know why?" she asked, and I was open ears. "Gabby was scheduled to have an abortion, and she's still healing from the aftermath, so let me tell you how it goes up here. This isn't floor two, baby. What I say goes. Follow my lead and keep up. I need all my tips, and I plan to get them," she said while I rolled my eyes.

"I can handle my damn self," I let it be known.

Usually, I would work on floor two aka middleville. They called it that because the niggas down there weren't too rich or too broke, They were stuck in the middle and had just enough money to tip. Since I was a favorite there, I got paid a little extra over the others. I also never had to start at the bottom, floor one. That was where the broke niggas were. You could expect the bare minimum of tips and watered-down drinks. All they were interested in was plotting and robbing niggas and trying to get on. They weren't popping bands down there. Floor three though, aka high stakes, was like heaven. I'd never worked up here, but I heard so many crazy stories. It was where the real ballers were, from athletes to drug dealers. They had them racks for real.

That was why I was confused when Montell told me I was working this floor. Nevertheless, I planned to use this advantage tonight. I had to make this shit count. Not only was this a beneficial opportunity for me, but I didn't know if Montell would continue to let me work up here.

"Hmm. Maybe so, but I run shit up here. So again, follow my lead," Marissa said, giving me the rundown. "Over there," she said, pointing her finger. "Those niggas like their liquor clear, nothing dark. And over there, they like to switch it up. Today is Tuesday, so they're only doing brown. They not really the talkative type. They like to drink and have a good time. That's it. You got it?" Marissa said, after going on for almost ten minutes.

"Yeah," I said, about to walk off until she jumped in front of me.

"Now… you're really ready." She adjusted my breasts for me so that they were more revealed. "Mhm, we getting real big tips tonight." She smiled.

I ran my fingers through my hair, and then got in my bag. When I was out on the floor, nothing else mattered. I had to have my eyes on the prize, and that was exactly what I was on as I approached the first table I saw. "You fellas know what y'all want to drink tonight?" I said, remembering Marissa saying they were the group who loved conversation and to switch it up sometimes.

"Damn, you gotta be new around here. I ain't seen you around ever," some guy said to me while he licked his lips sexually.

"Nah, it's just my first day working high stakes," I let

him know while he looked me up and down and licked his lips again. I was used to this shit, so I was unphased.

"What's yo' name, baby?" he asked while I tried so hard not to roll my eyes.

Marissa could read the annoyance on my face, so she nudged my shoulder for me to speak up.

"Ivy," I plainly spoke.

"That's sexy. I like it. What you doing after tonight though? I got a spot not too far from here," he said, grabbing my arm.

Once I felt his hands slide down to my ass was when I had to draw the line. "What the fuck are you doing? Nigga, don't you ever put yo' dirty ass hands on me. Fuck wrong with you?" I said, quickly pushing him off of me while his friends cracked up in the section.

"Ivy, cool the fuck down," Marissa told me while I ignored her.

I learned early on that I had to set boundaries when it came to these men. If I let them get away with the smallest shit, then next thing I'd know, they feel comfortable to do anything to me. Nah, I didn't get down like that. I respected myself.

"What's wrong with yo' homegirl? This bitch trippin' for no reason," the guy said.

"Bitch? The only bitch I see is yo' bum ass. Don't you ever put your hands on me again. I don't give a fuck who you claim to be, nigga," I said while Marissa pulled me back.

"Ayo, Rodney, chill the fuck out, nigga. We not pressed over no pussy over here. It's way too much of it in this world," another guy spoke from the corner with some girl on his lap. He was tall, dark, and handsome with the whitest teeth I'd ever seen.

"You right, Ty. Fuck that bitch," Rodney said while I squinted my eyes and was about to approach him again until Marissa grabbed me.

"We'll be right back." She smiled and pulled me away. "Ivy, what the fuck are you doing? You know how much them niggas pay when they step out? What did I tell yo' ass? Don't get in the way of my money. That's fuckin' Ty and his crew. Do I needa go get Montell?" she said while I rolled my eyes.

"I don't give a fuck. Ain't no nigga about to be touching on me. I'm not no damn stripper. I'm a bottle girl."

"Yeah, well, up here the lines get real blurred. Tighten up, bitch," she said through gritted teeth and then walked away.

*Fuck that section!* I didn't give a fuck how much they were blowing. At the end of the day, my respect came first. I would've gone back to floor two. In fact, I tried, but Montell's ass wouldn't allow it. I was stuck up here with a bunch of mothafuckas I didn't want to be around.

*Great.*

# Tyrell Zaire Dorsey

"Baby, you like my hair?" Vanessa asked me as she sat in my lap at Club Wishes. I was in the section with my niggas Rodney, Breeze, and some more niggas from the block. We usually came here from time to time. They had the best food, drinks, music, and, most importantly, the baddest females. We were regulars in this mothafucka, and that was known, hence, why we always got treated like royalty in here. Me and this club had a history that people didn't even know about.

"It's straight," I said, taking a drag from my blunt as I peeped the scenery.

To have been through the shit I had, it was a must to do two things when leaving the crib—one, keep that strap, and two, be cautious of your surroundings. That was the shit I lived by.

Vanessa smacked her lips. "You didn't even look at it, Ty." She pouted while I exhaled sharply. "Aye, don't blow my vibe in this bitch. I'm tryna chill tonight. Stop fuckin' up the vibe, V." I warned her.

Vanessa was cool. I'd been fucking her for about a year now, but we weren't on nothing serious. Whenever I called, she came through, and vice versa when I had the time. I was okay with our arrangement, and so was she.

I wasn't on anything serious with anybody, and it'd been that way since the beginning. I tried that relationship shit for a minute, and it was cool until fucking heavy turned into marriage talk. I had to cut my girl off for that shit. I wasn't the marrying type of nigga. I was too caught up in these streets. They were my true love. No doubt.

"Sorry, baby," she said, getting her shit together. "So what are you doing tomorrow?" she said, speaking up again. "I was thinking we could go out to eat and spend some time together," she said while I took a sip of my Hennessy straight.

"Let me check my schedule and get back to you," I said while she frowned and then put on a fake smile.

"Sounds great."

"Yo, Ty, look what mothafucka had the nerve to show his face tonight," Rodney said, getting my attention.

I turned to him, and my eyes averted to the crowd where I saw this nigga Mikey with some bitch. He was smiling all in her face, but what the fuck was there to be so happy about? He'd been avoiding me for weeks now, ever since I realized a few packs had been missing from my stash. Not only was he in control of that shit at the warehouse, but he answered to me every day. The fact that the nigga even thought it was cool to run off on me made my blood boil. Niggas knew not to cross me, ever. And if they did, they'd better be prepared for what came with that shit, always.

"Keep eyes on him for me."

"I got you." Rodney nodded. He was always there, since kids, making sure that we were good. Whatever I needed done, he did with no questions asked. He was a real one. That was why we both were out of the projects, living lavish and comfortable. We had the mindset that we weren't going back. That was my brother for life.

"Excuse me. Aren't you Aniya's cousin?" I heard Breeze say.

Looking straight ahead, I noticed he was talking to the bottle girl with the attitude from earlier. She wasn't a regular up here, because if she were, she wouldn't have dared thought to talk to Rodney the way she did. The nigga was a dog though for sure.

"I am," I heard her say back to him.

"Yeah, I thought that was you. I recognized you from her 'gram, but shit, can you tell her I ain't forgot about her and that my number still the same. My name Breeze," he told her while she smiled.

"Yeah, okay, I'll tell her for you, Breeze."

"'Preciate you," he said, handing her a whole three stacks, and then she walked away.

Once he looked at me and Rodney, we burst out

laughing.

"Man, fuck y'all niggas." He smacked his lips as we continued to laugh.

"Loverboy Breeze in the flesh." Rodney joked, and I shook my head.

"You still on that girl, huh?" I said, finishing off this blunt.

"Mind y'all business. You niggas wouldn't understand shit about soul ties," Breeze said while Rodney agreed.

"You damn right I wouldn't. Fuck I look like chasing a bitch or being tied to one? Could you imagine even settling for one piece of pussy? Fuck that shit." Rodney shook his head as he took down the rest of his 1942.

Vanessa rolled her eyes. "I'm going to the ladies' room," she said, quickly getting off of me.

I let her be. There was no need to sugarcoat shit with her anyway. She knew what it was.

"Watch yo' mouth when it comes to her. You already know I'm not going for no disrespect when it comes to Ni. I want all the smoke." Breeze stood while I sat back and watched them go back and forth.

"I ain't disrespect her ass. Shut yo' crybaby ass up. Going hard for a female who ain't hit you in how long? Nigga, we tryna school you."

Breeze was the youngest out the crew. He was only twenty-one, which meant he had so much more living to do. He had so much more to learn as well in this life, especially when it came to these women, but shit, I mean, he was grown enough to make his own choices, so if he wanted to be lovesick over his ex, then so be it. As long as it didn't get in the way of my bread, I was good. I must say it was amusing to see him so head over heels for ole girl. That wasn't my story to tell though.

"You can't school me on shit, bitch, but how to test positive for gonorrhea and to have multiple kids with multiple bitches. I'm out," he said, leaving the section.

I was in this bitch, nearly in tears from all the laughing I was doing. I could always count on Breeze for a good Thanksgiving clap back. He and Rodney stayed going back and forth, pure entertainment.

"Get off my dick, Breeze! And it was crabs, not gono, bitch!" Rodney shouted out loud.

Luckily, the music was blasting, but he clearly didn't give a fuck about the world knowing his health.

We stayed at Club Wishes for about another thirty minutes, and after that, I was ready to get the fuck. Closing time was right around the corner, and I didn't want to be here when that time came. Everybody knew mothafuckas wanted to pop their shit when the club ended. That was why I always made sure I was gone before closing.

"So you're coming home to me tonight?" Vanessa asked as we went down the elevator to the main floor.

"Should I?"I smirked while she proceeded to come closer to me.

"You should," she said, placing a single kiss to my neck.

"We'll see," I said, watching the elevator doors open. Truth be told, I already had it in my mind to slide through to her crib. My dick was harder than a rock from all of the alcohol I'd ingested, so Vanessa would definitely see me tonight.

"We will." She smiled cockily as we stepped foot outside.

"Remember what you asked me to keep eyes on? We got Mikey in the alley," Rodney said, approaching me quietly.

"Give me a minute," I let him know.

He nodded and went his way so I could finish up this conversation with Vanessa. It wasn't really anything else to say, but I needed to at least make sure she got to her car safely.

After I said my goodbyes to her, I went straight to the alley. I wasn't in the mood to do too much talking with Mikey, because I knew what it was. The nigga obviously had a death wish, and I was here to grant it for him.

I got closer to the alley and saw Rodney standing directly in front of Mikey, who didn't move a muscle off of the wall. A couple more niggas from the warehouse were present as well, but this was all on me. This shit was personal.

"What you on, Mikey?" I said, approaching him while he put his hands in his pockets and looked to the ground.

"You tell me, Ty."

The fact he couldn't even look me in my eyes told me he was guilty. I took eye contact very seriously. That was why nobody could lie to me. A person's eyes told it all.

"What's up with them missing packs, nigga? What? You thought we wouldn't notice or something, bitch ass boy?" Rodney said, immediately becoming aggressive. He was the hotheaded one, and violence was always his number-one answer to everything. I guess it had its pros and cons.

"Chill out, I got this," I said, telling Rodney to fall back. I had this shit under control as always. Maybe if I wanted a quick kill, I'd let Rodney do Rodney, but I wasn't on that right now. Things needed to go my way.

"This what this all about, bro? Some missing packs?" Mikey said, still avoiding eye contact. I laughed a little and rolled up my sleeves.

"Nah, Mikey," I said, slightly pushing Rodney out the way. "It's about loyalty," I spoke directly in front of him.

"Well then, you should know I've been loyal," he said while I turned away from him and laughed.

"Y'all hear this shit? Nigga said he been loyal. Since when did stealing from a man who put you on become loyal? Huh?" I said, turning back to Mikey, sending a single blow right to his jaw. "Ho ass nigga, don't ever play in my face like I'm some simp ass nigga. Fuck wrong with you?" I spat, watching him fall to the ground. "Get yo' ass up," I said, pulling him up from the ground by his jacket.

"Man, what you tryna do, Ty? You know I wouldn't do no shit like that, not to you.," he said, trembling like the coward he was born to be.

"Lie in my face one more time, and I won't spare you," I said, pulling out my gun and shoving it in his mouth. "Now I want you to listen to me real good 'cause I'ma only ask yo' bitch ass one time and one time only. Why did you decide to steal from me?" I said, about to remove the gun, but before I did, I had to refresh his memory. "Remember what I said."

He nodded slowly, and this time, I successfully removed the gun. "I know I'm responsible for inventory, and I should've called... I should've hit you, but you gotta believe me. I had nothing to do with that shit," he said while I shook my head and ran a hand down my face.

"Gone on home, Mikey, we'll talk about this later." I

said slowly backing away from him. Looking in his eyes, I saw nothing but fear. A few years back it might've stroked my ego, but now, I was immune to it all. I had nothing to prove to anybody because the way I moved spoke volumes for not just me, but every person I truly rocked with. I was that nigga in real life.

"Okay," he said, wiping both of his hands on his jeans.

If I wasn't mistaken, I saw a tear roll down his face. It blew my mind how he could allow hisself to shed those tears in front of me like it actually meant something. *The fuck was he crying for?* There was nothing solid about him, and we only had room for solid individuals. For that reason, Mikey had to go. It was simple—get rid of all dead weight. Anybody who stole from me, I had zero remorse for.

I could've beaten him down until his lying ass actually gave me some answers, but for what? I didn't have time to break a pussy nigga down. Besides, the truth always revealed itself. But as of tonight—tonight my patience was running thin.

Cocking my gun, I jumped in front of Mikey and fired two shots into his head. I took those shots from the front because I wasn't the type to shoot anyone while they weren't looking. I'd rather be direct. Just because he couldn't look me in my eyes and tell me the truth didn't mean I couldn't look him in his while I ended his life. Watching his body drop truly brought a huge smile to my face. I never had any thoughts to spare this fuck nigga.

"Get somebody to clean this shit up," I specifically told Rodney. Just when I was about to put my gun away, I spotted a shadow in a distance. It was dark as hell, but I was so big on my surroundings that I caught any and everything.

Our eyes met, and neither of us moved. It was a woman. I could tell. But who? Seeing sudden movement sent my body to full attack mode. Woman or not, I had to protect me and my business first.

Taking off running into her direction with my gun, I ran like my life depended on it. Fuck, it did. Whoever this was would have to answer to me. She was too damn fast on her feet. I didn't blame her considering what she just saw. Maybe she thought she was next. I started to bust at her just to make her stop, but by now, we were out in the open.

"Aye! Stop!" I shouted as I continued to chase her down the sidewalk. There was no way in hell I was catching up to her. I might've been a fit young nigga, but working out wasn't my thing. I was too heavy on the weed, and shorty had me chasing her down. Fuck, my lungs weren't set up for this. I was fucking tired.

Luckily, a car had stopped right in front of her, making

her fall to the ground. Stopping to catch my breath, I peeped it was Rodney.

"Get the fuck off of me!" she shouted while he grabbed her, and she started to swing wildly on him.

He pushed her back to the ground and pointed his gun at her. "Bitch, be quiet."

"Put that shit away. We don't need it," I said, interfering fast for obvious reasons. Rodney would've pulled that trigger, no questions asked.

"You good? I was just tryna talk to you," I said, looking down at the girl. This time, the light was on full display, so I was able to get a real good look at her, and when I did, I was surprised.

Here we go again. The bottle girl with the attitude.

"I'm fine, and I didn't see anything. Just let me go back to work please," she pleaded.

"If you didn't see anything, why'd you run, ma?" I asked, putting my gun away.

Rodney, on the other hand, kept his out. He just didn't have it aimed at her.

"I don't know." She shrugged.

"You know I got this superpower that allows me to know when somebody is lying to me, right? What did you see?" I asked, squatting in front of her while she tried to back away from me. "I'm not gon' hurt you." I assured her. "Just tell me what I want to know, and then we'll figure it out from there."

"What the fuck is there to figure out? I didn't see anything!" she yelled.

Rodney smacked his lips. "Man, Ty, let me off this hoe. Fuck is we sparing her ass for? I ain't got time for this shit," he said, aiming the gun at her.

She gasped and started to cry. "Please, don't. I have a son."

"Put yo' gun away. I ain't gon' tell you no more," I told Rodney.

He gave me a look and finally did so.

I sighed and shook my head, giving ole girl my full attention. "Shorty, I'm tryna help you out here, but you making it real hard for me. Talk," I said while she wiped her tears and let out a breath.

"I came outside to answer a phone call. Right after that phone call ended, I heard gunshots. It was dark, so I didn't see anything. I only ran for obvious reasons. I didn't want to be next," she said, looking me directly in my eyes. She was telling the truth.

"I believe you."

"Huh? Nigga, what? It's clear her ass lying. She knows

more, and if you don't want this shit coming back up to haunt us, you'd let me dead her right here, right now," Rodney spoke.

Right when I was about to speak up, the sound of sirens filled my ears. "Shit, we gotta go. Let's go," I said, helping the stranger off of the ground.

"I'm going back to work," she said, about to walk toward the building.

"Nah, you coming with me," I said, and her eyes got big.

"I-I can't. The club is literally right there. I'm good, see." She called herself trying to show me her physical appearance, but what about her mental? That was what was important.

"I wasn't asking. I was telling."

"Look, I know you don't know me, and I don't know you, but you have nothing to worry about. As far as I'm concerned, this night never happened. Just let me go," she said as the sirens grew louder.

"Fuck! We gotta go, and I mean right now. I know you hear that shit. They like less than five minutes away," Rodney said, looking over to me, but my eyes never left from the girl in front of me.

"Don't make me use this shit. I never miss my target,

ever," I said, aiming my gun at the ground and not at her. I didn't want to hurt her, but clearly, she needed some fire lit up under her ass.

She wasn't taking my kindness in, and I hardly gave that shit away, especially to a female I didn't know. It was best if she followed my orders. I didn't want to have to show her that other side of me.

"We all leaving together," I let her know one last time while I picked her phone up off the ground. "What's your name?"

"Ivy."

"Come on, Ivy."

Looking in my eyes, she didn't say another word. She got in the back of Rodney's Range Rover with me while he drove us away from all of the commotion.

"Where to?" Rodney said from the driver's seat.

"Drop us off at the crib," I told him, and he stopped the car and looked back at me.

"The crib? You really wanna take this bitch where you lay your head at?" he said.

Ivy shot her head up from her lap. "Call me a bitch again. I fuckin' dare you," She shouted, charging at Rodney, wildly hitting him in his head a few times.

"What the fuck? Ty, get this crazy ass girl off of me

before I put her ass down," Rodney complained.

Stepping in, I grabbed Ivy by her waist and sat her back down in her seat. "Chill the fuck out, Ivy."

"Don't tell me what the fuck to do," she said, pushing my hands off of her. "I wanna go home now. Take me home!" She kicked and screamed like a child.

"Okay, I had enough of her crazy ass," Rodney said, pulling out his gun. Clearly, that was his favorite thing to do.

"Everybody, shut the fuck up!" I barked. Irritated was an understatement. They were working a nigga's nerve. Emotions were high on Ivy's end, but I wasn't going to do this girl no harm. All she had to do was cooperate. And I couldn't leave Rodney in control. From his words to his actions, they were all reckless. I was her best chance. "Push this mothafucka, Rodney," I demanded him to do so, and he did.

The whole car ride to my crib, nobody said a word, and that was the way I liked it. Peace and fucking quiet. I needed time to think on how I was going to play this. However, I didn't trust Ivy. She was a stranger.

"What you need from me?" Rodney asked, finally pulling up to my spot.

"Give me a minute," I told him while he nodded and parked. "Come on," I said, looking over to Ivy, who had an unreadable expression on her face. I couldn't tell what she thought of me, but I could admit it did, in fact, bother me. Usually, I could read people, but when it came to Ms. Ivy, well, she was a different story.

She turned away from my direction for a good ten seconds, and I could've sworn she was talking to somebody, but no one was there. Without saying a word, she followed my lead.

"I'll be back," I told Rodney.

Unlocking my door, Ivy and I both stepped inside, with me in front. Things were just like I left them, so that was a good sign. "You good?" I said, taking a few steps forward and noticing Ivy stood there still.

"I wanna—"

"Go home," I said, finishing her sentence for her. "I know, and you will if you choose to cooperate. Sit, I'll be back," I said, not waiting for her to respond. I went upstairs to my room and then the bathroom to search for a first aid kit. Once I found it, I went back downstairs to find Ivy sitting on the couch with her head hung low.

The noise of my presence slightly frightened her, but once she realized what I had in my hand, she became a little calmer.

"Let me see your leg," I said, taking the seat next to her.

"Why?"

I shot her a confusing ass look. "Because yo' shit is scraped up pretty bad. You gon' let a nigga get you right or what?" I asked her.

She sighed and allowed me to assist her. She stuck her leg out for me to see while I grabbed it and placed it on my lap.

Looking at her kneecap, I saw the concrete did her some harm, but it wasn't anything too serious, just a little blood and a few cuts. She watched me intensively while I opened the alcohol pad. Right when I was about to apply it to her skin, she jumped a little.

"Don't tell me with a smart-ass mouth like yours, you scared of a little sting shorty." I laughed some while she rolled her eyes.

"I'm not."

"Good," I said, dabbing the alcohol pad on her cut while she bit her lip and moved a little. "That wasn't so bad, was it?" I asked, pulling out the ointment and Band-Aid.

"Why do you care so much anyways?"

"I don't know," I honestly spoke.

After I made sure she was straight. I told her to stay put while I went to chop it up with Rodney. It was a hassle because she was the hardheaded type, but after ten minutes of arguing, she finally agreed.

"Finally, nigga. You had me worried. I was finna come inside and do what I do best," Rodney said.

I shook my head. "You wanna use yo' gun so bad."

"Do," he said, and we both laughed.

"But on a serious note, I need you to make sure they took care of the body. We don't need no lose ends, so I need you to make sure everything is taken care of from witnesses, security footage, whatever. You know what to do."

Rodney was my right-hand man. He knew the ins and outs of this game just like me, and whenever I needed to handle shit like this, he was my go-to always. He had my back, and I damn sure had his.

"I got you, Ty, but shit, what we gon' do about that psychopath you holding hostage in there?" he asked, referring to Ivy.

"I got that under control. Just hit me first thing in the morning." I dapped him up.

"No doubt. I'm gon' get at you," he said, and I nodded, going back inside.

To my surprise, Ivy was still sitting in the same spot on the couch. I just knew she was going to try to run off somewhere, but I was wrong. Maybe she stayed because she knew I'd find her and possibly kill her, or maybe she stayed because she didn't believe I would harm her. I couldn't pin either one out.

"Here," I said, tossing her some sweats and a T-shirt from upstairs.

"Thanks, I guess."

"You're welcome, I guess," I retorted.

She cut her eyes at me and then disappeared. When she came back, she was dressed in the clothes I gave her. "Since you won't let me leave right now, how about you run the rules and regulations by me so I can agree and be on my way," she said, crossing her arms.

I smirked and looked her up and down. "No rules or regulations. You didn't see anything, right?"

"Ty, cut the bullshit and let me know what's up. You aren't gonna kill me, are you? So why am I still here? Why even bring me to your damn house?" she asked, approaching me in an angry manner.

"Ivy, move around," I said, trying to stop her before she did something she would regret.

"Or what?" she said, continuing to walk up on me.

I knew what I said, and I meant that, but never would I go for any disrespect, especially when I could've offed her myself. There was no need to even be hostile in my eyes. I spared her. *You welcome.*

"Or you can see that other side of me. Your fuckin' choice," I said, grabbing her arms and pinning her against the wall roughly.

We stood there for a good minute, staring each other down, until Ivy decided to look away.

"I'ma tell you how's it going down, even though I know you already know. Tonight never happened, you didn't see anything, and you don't know nothing. Fuck it, you don't even know me. You was never here and don't know where I stay. I don't gotta tell you what's gon' happen if I find out you opened your mouth. Believe me when I tell you, I'm a man of my word. I will find you if I have to. No matter where you go or who you run to. I will get to you if I have to. Understood?" I broke it down to her.

If she was frightened by a threat, then she could only imagine what would take place if I found out she disobeyed me. I wasn't the type to kill just to kill, but if I had to, I would, simple as that. Ivy didn't seem like a threat at all, and despite everything that went down tonight, maybe she was an okay female. I just hoped, for her sake, she wouldn't do anything stupid with the little information she knew about me, because then, I would have to retaliate in a negative way. Taking her away from her child and everything else she had in her life.

"Yeah," she simply stated.

I nodded and let her go. "Coo'. I'll take you back to the club. Let's ride," I said, leading the way. She was right on my tail too. I knew she wanted to hurry up and get away from my crazy ass.

Going into my garage, I grabbed the keys to my 2020 midnight-blue Lambo truck, and we got in.

As expected, the whole car ride was quiet with the exception of the radio. I never listened to that shit either, but the silence was killing me. Even if I wanted to speak up, my head wouldn't allow me to. There was no need to be friendly with her. She'd already got enough of my kindness tonight. Others couldn't say the same.

"Hello?" I said, picking up my ringing phone. It was going on four in the morning, so it couldn't be anybody but the block or Vanessa.

"Where are you? I've been calling you," Vanessa said while I put her on speaker and set the phone down.

"What's up? What you need?" I said, purposely ignoring her asking me about my whereabouts. *The fuck she thought this was?* Only female I was answering to was my mother.

"I need you, baby," she said.

Ivy started to cough uncontrollably loudly. Shooting her a look, she silently cleared her throat. "Oops. My bad."

Something told me her ass did that on purpose. From the little time I spent with her, I was starting to feel her out. She was petty as hell for sure.

"Ty, who are you with?" Vanessa said, catching an attitude.

"What?" I said, shooting the phone a confusing look like it was her or something. It just blew me. There she was again questioning a nigga.

"You heard me."

"Aye, I don't know who the fuck you talking to, but you know better than to question me on some lame shit like that, V," I said and heard her smack her lips.

"It's not even like that, but at the same time, I'm not finna let you disrespect me either."

"Go hit another nigga to come fuck you then. What you on my line for?" One thing about it, I wasn't arguing with a female that wasn't mine, and only one female had that title before, but that was more than a few bodies ago, and I've been out here living life, wearing protection though, of course.

"I'm not on that type of time, and you know that."

"I don't know shit. If I come through, I do. If I don't, then I don't," I said, hanging up in her face. She called back a couple of times, but every time, I ignored her. She'd hit me later on apologizing, and I might decide to fuck around if not oh well.

"Wow… tuh, niggas," I heard Ivy mumble.

"You got something you wanna say to me?" I said, looking over to Ivy while I drove with one hand.

"Nope," she plainly spoke.

I smirked, then licked my lips. "Figures."

"What's that supposed to mean?" she said, catching an attitude just like Vanessa.

I didn't know what was up with these females tonight, but they were really blowing me. "Just what the fuck I said. I ain't stutter around this bitch," I said while she exhaled sharply and then got quiet. "Yeah, alright then," I said, continuing to drive. The sooner I got her and her attitude out my whip, the better.

We pulled up to Club Wishes in less than twenty minutes. Things were quiet and cleared out for the most part, with an exception of a few cars. That was the way it needed to be. I was sure the cops probably asked questions, but I wasn't worried at all. Things would be taken care of around here like they always were. The only thing I wanted to do was get back to the crib and take my ass to bed. I didn't picture my night ending like this, but it was like that sometimes.

Ivy undid her seat belt and was about to get out until I grabbed her arm. She looked at my hand around her arm and then my face.

"What?"

"Here," I said, putting her phone in her lap.

"How sweet of you," she said in a sarcastic tone.

"You know what? I'm really tired of yo' ungrateful, stuck-up ass."

"Yeah, well, luckily, we never have to see or come in contact with each other again," she said, opening up my car door.

"Tuh, luckily," I responded while she slammed my door hard as hell and then walked away.

I watched her until she disappeared into the club and that was that. I wasn't fucking with her crazy ass.

# *Ivy*

Three weeks later

"Kacey, please don't embarrass me today in here. Be a big boy and get your hair cut for mommy, and then afterwards, we can go get some ice cream okay?" I said, walking hand in hand with him to the barbershop. It was a shame I had to bribe my son sometimes just to behave, but I had to do what I had to do.

"Okay, Mommy," he said.

I sighed of relief. Kacey had a bad habit of not wanting to be around strangers for too long, even if his cousin owned the damn shop. He was attached to me, not just mentally, but sometimes physically. If I wasn't in his presence, then he was throwing a fit in some way. Kids always wanted to embarrass parents in front of people.

"Damn."

"Look at her fine ass."

"She know she bad. All I need is ten minutes with her."

I heard a few men say as I entered into Marie Cutz. They were always like this when I showed up here, thirsty and lusting over what they couldn't have—me.

Sammy, my younger cousin, named his shop after our grandmother once she passed away. She believed in him just

51

like her other grandchildren. I found it to be the sweetest thing how God kept her alive so that she could make it to the grand opening. Two days later, she was gone.

Me, Sammy, and Jai were the product of Grandma Marie and Grandpa Leon. We made sure to spend as much time as we could together and to stay close no matter what. They were my cousins but more like my siblings. Same with Aniya. She was my cousin from my father's side, and even though I had no contact with him, it didn't really make a difference. We were all family, and we were all close.

"Look who it is. Little ass Ivy. I'll be with y'all in a minute," Sammy said while I walked over to him and mushed his head.

"Boy, stop playing with me. I'm yo' big cousin, remember that," I said, and he smacked his lips. "Yeah by four funky ass months. Don't get it twisted," he said, and we both laughed.

"Whatever. And let me find out I gotta go find another barber. I set my son's appointment for two o'clock on the dot. It's going on two now, and you got somebody in the chair," I said, just talking shit.

"Can't nobody get my little cousin right but me. Don't be having him cheat on his barber at a young age just because I'm running a little behind schedule."

"You're so aggravating. We're gonna go sit down until you're done. Come on, Kacey," I said, taking his hand while we sat in some chairs to the side. Looking around, I couldn't be prouder of Sammy. It was so nice in here from the clean floors to the stations. Sammy was a proud black business owner at the age of twenty-three who never forgot where he came from, and he had the pictures around the shop to prove it.

"Alright, let me get my baby cousin right," Sammy said after about twenty minutes.

"Next time, don't be having us waiting. We royalty around here," I said, grabbing Kacey's hand and sitting him in the chair.

"Shut up. I don't even make y'all pay."

"But I still do though," I said, moving my neck from side to side.

"I don't know how you deal with her, Kacey," Sammy told him and they both laughed. "Whatever. Let me go get his tablet so he can be still. I left it in the car," I said, going outside real quick.

As soon as I stepped foot out there, the heat snuck up on me. It wasn't too bad in Miami, but I was a fall type of girl. With the many looks I could pull off to the weather, it was just a vibe in my eyes.

I grabbed Kacey's tablet from the back seat and then locked the doors back.

"Ivy," I heard my name being called from afar. I started to ignore it just because I wasn't trying to be bothered today, but they just kept calling me.

Stopping in my tracks, I saw exactly who it was—my ex-boyfriend, Q.

"You gon' act like you don't hear me? What you on?" he asked, approaching me with this smirk mixed with a little smile. His whole demeanor screamed cocky with a whole lot of money. I never fucked on a broke nigga ever. For some, that didn't mean anything, but for me, it meant everything.

"What you want, Q?" I said, meeting him in the middle.

"Shit, I can't speak to you now? That's what we on?" he said while I rolled my eyes.

"We talking, aren't we?"

"You tell me."

"I'm not about to play with you."

Q was full of games, too many to be exact. That was why I had to cut him off completely. I spent two toxic ass years being with him. It came with a lot of shit though. I was only seventeen, fucking with one of the most-known D boys Miami had to offer. Everywhere that man breathed, I wanted to be, from the block to the club.

He spoiled me, bought me what I wanted, took me outta town on the regular, but he also took my virginity, my heart, and loyalty and ran with it. I wasn't the type to dwell on the past, but I knew for a fact I made the right choice when I left him alone. I mean, there was no bad blood between us. I just moved on. I was a mother now, and he was a father of two with two different baby mamas. It could be more, but who knows?

"What you mean? You look good though," he said, eyeing me down, from my white toes, to my thighs, to the revealed part of my breasts, all the way to lips and eyes. There wasn't anything shy about Q, and I meant that in all aspects. His approach to be forward was what got me caught up with him too many times. He had my young ass really thinking I was in love, crazy. Right after I broke up with him, I got with Rashad. That situation wasn't always the best either, but I was blessed to have Kacey.

"Thank you."

"You're welcome. What you been up to?" he asked, running his hand over his curls. The fresh line up told me he'd just gotten his hair cut. I was over here admiring his appearance just like he was with me. He was wearing a fresh white tee with a pair of True Religion jeans and some Air

Force Ones. He wore a few gold chains and a Rolex on his wrist that complemented his light skin. Q had the bag for sure, and I was convinced that would never change.

"Working," I said, keeping it brief for many reasons. He didn't need to know my business or feel like he could work his way back into my life. I didn't need the headache or distraction.

"Oh yeah? You still at Club Wishes?" he asked, and I nodded my head. "That's what's up. I know yo' nigga be hating, not wanting us to talk on some lame shit, but you know you my baby for life. Fuck the extra shit, Ivy. We for life."

It was just like Q to talk his shit. He had a mouthpiece on him, and if I was still seventeen, I'd be right with him, running the streets and thinking my shit didn't stink.

"Mhm," I simply stated. He didn't even need to know that I was single and wasn't fucking with Rashad. The two of them did have their little beef a few years back over me.

When Q found out I was with Rashad, he just had to make a scene, even after all he put me through with all the lying and cheating. They ended up running into each other at a party one night, and shit popped off. Q tried to kill Rashad.

"You know I still love you right? I'm gon' always love you, and if you need anything, I got you. Matter fact," he said, digging in his pocket at pulling out a wad of cash. "Here," he said, calling himself handing it to me.

From the look on my face, he knew that was a wrong move. "Q, you know me better than to try some shit like this. The day I take some money from a nigga that isn't mine, hell might as well freeze over."

"Oh, I forgot you the independent type now." He smirked and shook his head.

"Call it what you want."

"Q," I recognized one of his guys from the block shout. I knew what that meant. He had to go. Probably get into some shit that would get him in trouble.

"Here I come, G," he said, looking over to the guy and then back at me. "I'ma see you around. Hit me for whatever," he said, about to walk away.

"Be careful, Quinton," I spoke.

He turned back and smiled. "Always baby."

I wasn't in love with Q, but that didn't mean I wanted his time on this earth to be cut any time soon. Q was in the streets heavy though, and we all knew where that could lead you eventually.

"What took you so long? I thought I had to come out there with my belt 'cause you wanted to be fast," Sammy said.

I ignored him. "Here, baby," I said, handing Kacey his tablet and headphones.

"Thank you, Mommy."

I smiled and sighed. "What you been up to, Sammy, besides getting on my nerves?" I asked my cousin.

"Making this money and trying to stay out the way," he said, all focused and whatnot.

I started not to even have a conversation with him while he cut Kacey's hair because if he fucked my child up it was going to be a problem. I had faith in him though. Almost everybody in Miami went to him to get their hair cut.

"I'm proud of you. This is some real boss shit. You're so young but making big moves. You did a whole one eighty."

Like many of black teenage boys, Sammy did sell drugs fresh out of high school, but that only lasted awhile because my grandpa beat his ass down so bad when he found out what his grandson was doing. Sammy didn't touch outside for a month straight. Our grandparents didn't play. Sammy told me, out of his mouth, he was good at the drug game, but more was expected from him, so he went to find better. He used to cut his own hair and my grandpa Leon's, and the rest is history.

"'Preciate that. You know I got a baby on the way," he said.

My eyes got wide. "What? With who? Why am I just now finding out? Damn, are you even ready, Sammy?"

"Would you stop throwing all these questions at me, Ivy? Shit, you acting like I don't got a pot to piss in or something." He shot a look at me and then shook his head.

"My bad. I'm just curious," I admitted.

"Nosy." He tried to correct me.

"Shut up and answer my questions, ugly."

"Her name is Ari. We been fuckin' around for about eight or nine months now. She said she wanted to wait until she was at least three months for people to know." He let me know.

"Okay. You've said everything except if you're ready to have a baby and you really love this girl."

"Because I'm not. I know that for a fact, but I'm not no flaw ass nigga either. I'm gon' take care of my responsibilities as a man because I know what it's like to not have a father. A baby is innocent."

"And you don't love her, Sammy?" I questioned him while he shook his head.

"I'm not in love with her, but one day I will be."

"How do you know that?"

"I just do."

"Wow." I shook my head in disbelief. "You tell your big sister?"

"Hell no I didn't tell Jai yet. I'm gon' do that later on.

But I mean, what can she say? I'm a grown ass man with his own crib, cars, and business."

"True," I said, agreeing.

"Well, I'm happy for you. A baby is truly a blessing, but it won't be easy I'm telling you now." Even though Sammy didn't have to carry the baby, he still needed to put in the time and effort. I remember, from the time I found I was pregnant with Kacey, I was in shambles. I kept telling myself I wasn't ready, and all the people in my ear telling me what to do wasn't making it any better.

I made the right decision though, and couldn't anybody tell me differently. Rashad was there every step of the way with me from contractions to delivery. However, I did suffer postpartum depression after giving birth. That was when things got rocky and the cheating occurred. Those flashbacks still gave me chills sometimes.

I was in a dark place, and he tried to be there for me, but I pushed him away, practically right into another bitch's bed. I blamed myself, and it took me a while to get out that phase. Now I knew I couldn't excuse that shit, because if he really loved me, he would've stayed loyal to me. Still, in the past I took him back. I just never want to have to deal with none of that again. Kacey was my one and only child, and that was the way I wanted to keep it.

"So I've heard. Thanks though. I know to call you for any and everything." He joked, and I rolled my eyes playfully.

"Yeah, and I might answer."

"Don't do that," he said while I laughed.

"Anyways, when are we going to meet this girlfriend of yours? I say you bring her to the barbecue today. It's a perfect idea." I thought.

"Says who? Ari not my girlfriend. and I'm damn sure not bringing her to that ghetto ass function," he said while I burst out laughing.

"It is not gonna be ghetto."

"Shit, Jai bringing the whole hood out for her nigga. I'll pass," he said while I shook my head. "So you not coming?"

"Hell yeah I'm sliding through for my nigga Kordell. Five years way too long, but my baby mama won't be in attendance. Fuck that."

"So when am I gonna meet her then?" I needed to know the girl who was carrying my future baby cousin.

"I don't know. I'll let you know though." He winked and smiled.

"Sammy, I'ma really choke you out," I said, and he laughed.

"Get out my business, Ivy. What's up with you and that

nigga Rashad? How 'bout that," he said, now all in my business.

I wouldn't dare get into all of that with him, so I didn't know why he asked. He really didn't even want to know. Any time Jai and I had girl chat, he would move around fast. He left spilling tea to the females.

"Nothing at all."

He laughed. "Yeah, it better be that way 'cause if I find out it's a problem, I want all the smoke. Family first."

"Family first," I repeated after him.

That was our motto. We made a pact that we wouldn't be like our parents and their failed relationships with each other. I wasn't anything like my mother, and Jai and Sammy were nothing like their father. We were going to love one another through whatever, no matter if we got on each other's nerves. We were all we had.

After Kacey finished getting his hair cut, as promised, I took him to get some ice cream, and then we went to Jai's house. She wanted me to come over and help set up for Kordell's welcome home party. He got home yesterday, and they had a small and intimate dinner, but today, she was bringing the whole hood out for her man in Sammy's voice. I had to laugh just thinking about it.

Pulling up to Jai's crib, I always found a way to be

amazed, even though I'd been over here a million times. I could never get tired of seeing her fancy ass crib. She and Kordell shared a two-story five-bedroom home together with a pool and basketball court. It was so upscale that it was in a gated community. They had nice cut grass, a four-door garage, statues, and a whole water fixture out front. These were house goals.

"Mommy, can we go swimming in cousin Jai's pool?" Kacey said while we walked hand in hand to the front door.

"Later on, we can."

"Okay. Can I call my Daddy too?"

"Yes, wait until we get inside," I said, opening up the door. I knew it'll be unlocked.

The smell of food hit my nose from the outside, so I could only imagine what it was like inside. A few people were already over decorating, but the party didn't start for another hour or so.

"Hey, Ivy," everybody spoke.

"Hi," I said, giving a few hugs out. "Where is Jai?" I asked, looking around.

"Chile, upstairs with Kordell. You can't keep the two of them apart. Five years too long," Kordell's mom said as I immediately started to crack up. We all knew what they were up to, but I wasn't mad at that at all. Jai needed all the dick she missed out on. Thank God Kordell was home because Jai could be a grumpy bitch sometimes.

"I'm not mad at that," I said.

"Me either. I want me some grandkids. I wish the twins would bring me some right now. I'll put my foot in they ass," Ms. Glenda said referring to her younger twin boys, making me laugh. They were only eighteen.

"Y'all got everything set up?" I asked, putting Kacey on my hip while we walked to the back of the house.

"Just about. The food should be done soon. We got the cake. I just need help putting up some decorations, but I'll let the men do that. You want something to drink, baby?" she said, taking a seat on the sofa.

"No, I'm fine," I said, looking down at Kacey, who held me tightly while he rested his head on my chest. We were stuck like glue. He would forever be my baby.

"Okay, so how have you been?" Ms. Glenda said, lighting up here cigarette.

"Can't complain. That's not my style," I said, and she chuckled.

"I know that's right. I seen your mama the other day at the grocery store," she said.

I rolled my eyes. We still weren't really speaking like that. I just couldn't stand her attitude and slick comments. She really hated me, and I had no idea why. I was her only child, her only daughter… I would think she would do her best with loving me.

I was just tired. I'd tried everything from trying to communicate to offering therapy, but nothing worked. It hurt like hell, but I couldn't sulk in sorrow for too long. I had to get back up and make it happen. Still, I was tired of it all. Her energy was so damn dark, and I didn't want Kacey to feel any of it. That was why I hadn't been home in a week. Me and Kacey either stayed at his dad's or with Jai but Jai mostly because Rashad was quick to get the wrong impression. When I slept over, I stayed in the guest room or on the couch.

I needed to get my own place like yesterday, but a part of me felt drawn to that house. Would I ever have the courage to leave?

"Something is wrong with that woman." She shook her head and blew smoke. "But that's my friend. I'm praying for you both. She'll come around one day, Ivy," she said, looking over to me. "But until then, you just keep on making it."

"I'm gon' do more than just make it, Ms. Glenda. Trust me," I said, looking down at Kacey and kissing his forehead repeatedly.

"Hi, cousin," Jai said, coming over to me with a huge smile on her face. I hadn't seen her this damn happy in a while.

"Hey. Did you wash your hands?" I said, putting some space between us.

"Girl, I just got out the shower. Stop playing," she said, giving me a big hug while she kissed Kacey. "He's so attached. Kacey!" she said, tickling him while he laughed but never let me go. "What y'all talking about?" she said, sitting in the middle of us. She knew she were way too thick for all of that. Jai and I were two years apart and favored each other. She just was thicker and a little darker than me. Hell, everything on her was bigger than me, from ass to breasts. She was a true beauty.

"Nothing important," I let it be known.

"Mmm, I'm hungry. Hopefully everybody is on time. You talked to Sammy?"

"Yeah, we just left from up there. He said he was coming," I said, making sure I left the part about him having a baby on the way out. He could tell his big sister on his own.

"Let me go make sure they doing what I need them to do. Come on, Kacey, you can come play with the other kids?" Ms. Glenda said, standing up.

"You wanna go play in the pool? Go with Grandma Glenda," I told him while he happily got down. He didn't like too many people, but Ms. Glenda was the closest thing to a mother I had though my mother was still on this earth.

"I want you to come," Kacey said, patting my thigh.

"In a minute. I promise." I kissed his cheek, and he left with Ms. Glenda.

"Where your swimsuit at? This a pool party," Jai said, noticing I had on regular clothes. I was still wearing my lime-green overall romper with my brown faux fur slides.

"I'll find something upstairs. I got too many clothes up there."

"True, but bitch, you look cute with your little ponytail and baby hairs. I see you with your Fendi bag. Come through, Ivy Marie," she said, gassing me up.

"Jai, hush. How you feel?"

She sighed and then spoke up. "Overwhelmed and happy at the same damn time. I missed Kordell so damn much that it killed me inside. Ivy, you know that," she said.

When I looked at her, I saw fear before anything, but I couldn't understand why. Her man was home. What wasn't there to be happy about? I remember when they sent Kordell away like it was yesterday. He had got out on bond but was on house arrest until he went back in. The whole time, Jai stayed at home with him. We couldn't even get her to go up the street with us.

Kordell didn't miss a beat. Valentine's Day, Christmas, birthdays, even the New Year, Jai was sent a gift from him, and he was locked up. He supported her financially and mentally while she stayed down the whole time. I commended her for her strength.

"Jai, you held it down."

"But I'm not trying to again," she said, and I shot her a weird look.

"What do you mean?"

"I feel like there's something he isn't telling me," she said, scooting closer to me. "Like he misses his old life and wants to get back to it," she said while I caught on.

"Damn." Kordell pushed drugs. That was the reason they had half of the shit they did, but I guess Jai thought when he came home things would be different.

"Don't assume, just ask," I said, placing my hand on her thigh.

"I will. Just not right now. Right now, all I want to do is enjoy time with the family. Plus, he's too busy trying to put a baby in me for me to even get two words out."

"I know y'all been fuckin' like rabbits." I laughed with her.

"We have. All night last night to the morning. Little does he know, I'm not having any kids any time soon. What Nicki say? Ain't pushing out his baby 'til he buy the rock. I gotta be his missus first if anything," she said, surprising me a little.

"Good luck with that."

"Who needs luck when you got birth control?" she said tapping her arm, and I gasped.

"Bitch when did you have time to do this?" I wondered.

"Two weeks ago. What? Bitch, you thought I wouldn't be prepared. I knew my nigga was gonna come home and be on me like white on rice."

"Does he know?"

"No."

"You know you needa tell him. Got that man cumming in you nonstop just to get nothing in the end. Gon' have him thinking he shooting blanks or something," I said, and she laughed. "I'm serious, Jai."

"I will, eventually." She shrugged.

"What's up, Ivy?" Kordell said, coming out of nowhere with this deep ass voice, making me jump a little. It seemed like he got taller and more buff. This man looked like he'd break a nigga in half with no hesitation if someone was to try him.

"Hey, Kordell. Welcome home." I stood, giving him a hug.

"'Preciate that, family. Where little man at?" he asked,

letting me go.

"With your mom."

"Damn, how old is he now?"

"Three and all about me." I smiled, and he did the same.

"That's what's up. Gotta have a few of my own soon," he said, looking at Jai while she innocently smiled.

"For sure." I sat back down.

She needed to tell him the truth, soon.

"Hey, my handsome son. To what do I have the pleasure?" my mom said, meeting me at her front door. I never called when I came and before I could even knock on the door. She was always there to greet me. I didn't know how she did it, she just always knew.

"What's up beautiful? How are you?" I said, giving her a hug.

Her hugs were the best. They made a nigga feel like all the wrong he did in the world would never catch up to him. From birth, her arms were a safe haven for me, but I knew they couldn't always save me. I was a grown man who was responsible for his own actions, and at the end of day, she knew that as well.

"I'm doing good. I did some yoga earlier today, baby," she said.

I couldn't help but laugh. "Oh yeah? How did that go for you?" I said, following her into the kitchen.

"Pretty good. You know your mother will always have it," she said, flipping her natural tresses around. My mother was beautiful and didn't look a day over twenty-five. She was fly whenever she stepped out the crib, but even when she was inside on her natural shit, she was a sight to see.

She had me at sixteen, so we grew together in many ways. Before anything, she was my mother, but I viewed her as a friend as well. She knew me best and always kept it real with me.

"I'm already knowing," I said, taking a seat at the bar. "You didn't cook nothing today? I don't smell anything," I said, looking around the kitchen.

"No, I went out for lunch."

"With who?" I quickly spoke up, and she rolled her eyes playfully and smiled.

"Tyrell Zaire Dorsey, I'm not worried about you," she said, putting some fresh water in a vase for her flowers.

"And who sent you flowers? It wasn't me, because I know to get you sunflowers all the time."

"I bought them myself. Any more questions? I—don't answer that." She laughed, and I shook my head.

"Alright, you not grown," I told her as she waved her hand.

"I'm not about to play with you, boy. You still haven't told me why you came either," she said, putting on a kettle of water on for some tea.

She stayed making me eat clean and drink a lot of tea. She even made me keep some sage at the crib. My mother was a very spiritual woman, and it'd been that way since I could remember. I didn't grow up in the church house or nothing like that, but my mom was a firm believer in God. I was too. It was just you could say her faith was a whole lot stronger than mine.

"I missed you."

"I missed you too, son. I get so lonely in this big house by myself," she complained.

"I bet you wished you had more kids times like this," I said as she sighed.

"Tell me about it because Lord knows your stubborn ass won't give me any grandkids any time soon."

"Whatever God has planned for me, right?" I said, looking up at her.

"Yeah and I've been talking to Him lately. I've been praying for a grandbaby. Twins," she said.

I coughed. "Twins? You showing out, Mama."

"How? I'm in this upscale four-bedroom home, and it's just me."

"I got a room here too."

"Yeah, and it's not like you use it either." She was right. The only time I used it was for the holidays. Every last holiday, I spent a night, but I also visited her at least four times a week. We talked every day though.

"So I'll move in with you." I joked.

"And have all those fast things all up in here like high school? Tuh, I think not," she said, taking the seat next to me. "What's worrying you, Tyrell? You know you can tell me anything. I'm here always," she said, placing her hands on each side of my face.

I sighed and put my head down. I didn't even come here for anything serious, but it was like every time I came to see my mama, I grew guilty inside for all the wrong I was doing in this world. It wasn't a secret to my mother that I was in the streets. She told me every night she would pray that I left them streets alone, but that prayer hadn't come true yet, and I didn't know if it would ever come to that. I was prepared to die in these streets alone.

"I told you I just missed you," I said, and she huffed and kissed my forehead.

"Boy, pray with me real fast," she said while I nodded.

The whole time she said a prayer to God, my mind was on one thing and one thing only—Mikey. I would kill with no hesitation, but that didn't mean it didn't haunt me from time to time. Every time I closed my eyes, I saw his blood. He deserved his death, but I didn't deserve the constant reminder of his disloyal ass. Fuck him.

Sometimes I wondered was there even a place in heaven for a heartless ass nigga like me, but I figured, since

God and my mother were like best friends, He would make some room for a real one.

"Amen," my mother said.

I repeated after her. "Amen."

"There. Whatever is heavy on your heart is now in God's hands," she said, holding my hands close to her heart.

"Thank you, Mama," I replied genuinely.

"You're welcome, love. What are you doing tomorrow?" she said, getting up and making her way back to the opposite side of the kitchen.

"I don't know. Whatever you need me for, I'll make time." I was always going to move around my schedule for her.

"I wanted to go put some flowers on your daddy's grave. If you're up for it, I would like you to come with me," she said, looking at me for answers I almost couldn't give her.

"I can't. Maybe after you leave, we can have lunch or something though," I said, and she sighed, then smiled.

"Oh, I would love that."

I nodded my head. "Okay."

My pops died when I was just thirteen years old. It'd been over ten years that I had to live without him, and it still fucked me up. It fucked me up so much that I could never go visit his grave, even as a child. My mother begged me to go, but I couldn't do it, feeling like if I stepped foot in the graveyard, then it'd be too real for me, so I stayed away. Some days I still believed that I would wake up from this nightmare. Wishful mothafuckin' thinking.

Just like me, my pops was in the streets. He was damn good at it too. So good we were able to live a lavish life. Whatever I wanted, he provided for me and my mother both. I had the whole block wanting to be my friend just because of all the good shit I had as a kid. When Future said drug money would buy you what you want, he was telling the damn truth.

When my pops died, I made sure I was able to maintain our lifestyle. I got a few jobs, even though I didn't have to. I just wanted to make sure my mama didn't have to want for nothing. My pops left us plenty of racks, some money we ain't even touched yet. I just had this mentality to never go broke, and in the drug game, you never did, not when it was me. That was why I started hustling.

She knew I was sensitive when it came to his death, especially because we didn't know who killed him, so she changed the subject. "You really want me to cook you something? I can fry you some chicken. I took it out last night but changed my mind on cooking it."

"Nah, it's okay, Mama. I'll eat when I leave here."

"Mmm okay…" she dragged out.

"What you about to do though, lady?"

She sighed and ran her fingers through her fresh blow out. "I don't know. Probably watch me some *Greenleaf* or something," she said, making me laugh.

"I'm on season two I think."

"It's good, ain't it?" she asked me, laughing while I nodded.

"Yeah."

"See? I told you. That damn Zora is a fool. She need her a good smack across the head."

"Facts, 'cause I wish my daughter would."

My mama put me on all the TV shows, and when I had the time, I'd tune in. Some shit I just couldn't fuck with though, but I had all the streaming sites at the crib on all my TVs. I had everything anyone could think of at the crib just because I had the money.

Just like my mother, it was only me at my place, yet I had plenty of room. Half the time, having a family didn't sound so bad, but then I'd start to think of my lifestyle. It wasn't that I didn't want to have a family and kids, but could I? A family came with too many responsibilities. Then it was like would I feel obligated to leave the streets? Would the mother of my kids want me to? I couldn't handle all of that right now.

I owed my mama some grandkids though. I had to give

her some before either of us left this earth. Just thinking about her excitement made me smile inside. If I took that route, I had to find the perfect one. The females I fucked weren't wifey material. They were good for one thing. As soon as I caught my nut, I was ready for them to move the fuck around.

Vanessa was number one on that list if anything. We fucked around heavy, and I didn't mind her staying at the crib as long as she wasn't on that clingy and annoying shit. Lately, she'd been showing her ass though, and that was why I had to quit fucking with her for a few days.

I stayed at my mother's crib for a good thirty more minutes, and she was sure to make me drink all of my tea. Now I was off to my next destination, my nigga Kordell's welcome home party. He did five years and got charged for manslaughter. Luckily his lawyer did his thing because they were trying to give him life at the very least.

When he went away, he didn't want none of his niggas to write or visit him. I wasn't stepping in a prison no way, but I did miss my dawg. He took that time like it was nothing, and I salute him for that. Kordell was solid from the jump. We grew up in the same hood, so we would kick it almost every day. He was somebody who I could count on to keep it real. It was only right I showed up for him.

Pulling up to his crib, I couldn't even find a parking

spot. It was that crowded. I mean, I wasn't surprised really, because the whole hood knew Kordell, and when you were solid, mothafuckas fucked with you the long way.

I parked my car a few houses down and then went inside. They had the whole neighborhood smelling like barbecue, and I was ready for a plate. Ms. Glenda could throw down the way my mama didn't like to. I was going to leave this bitch on a full stomach for sure.

"Hey baby," Ms. Glenda said as soon as I walked in.

"Hey, good to see you," I said, giving her a hug.

"You too. You staying out of trouble, Tyrell? I hope so."

"Always." I smirked.

"Boy, I'ma beat yo' ass," she said, pinching my cheeks, and I laughed. "Everybody is in the backyard, including Kordell."

"Alright, let me go find him," I said as she nodded, and we went our separate ways.

"My nigga, Ty. What the fuck is up?" Kordell said, finding me before I could find him.

"Damn, nigga, welcome home. You 'bout big as hell," I said, giving him a bro hug.

"Yeah, so try me, nigga, and I'll knock yo' head off yo' shoulders." He joked.

"Nah, dawg, I ain't even tryna go there with yo' Terry Crews–looking ass," I said, and he laughed, but I was dead ass serious. It was obvious what he spent his time doing away—lifting.

"Wasn't shit else to do in there but work out, read, and try not to kill a mothafucka," he said, smoking on a black.

"I feel you, but now you home. You ready to get back to the paper?"

"Ready as a fiend anticipating a fix," he said, and I laughed some.

"Nigga, you ready for real then."

We both laughed and took a seat at a table. "What you been on foo'? I know you still on a money-making mission."

"Always that. Things going good. Me, Rodney, and Breeze got the drug game on lock. You can step in if you want to. You know I got a spot for you on the team," I let him know.

Before Kordell went in, he was in the same boat as me with hustling, but over the years, a lot of shit changed, a lot of niggas were dead, and new opportunities presented themselves. If he wanted to get down with me and my niggas, he could. I trusted him and was sure he would catch on quick. It wasn't like he was new to this shit.

He sighed and scratched his chin. "I don't even know if that's what I'm tryna do though," he said, surprising me some. I thought for sure he would always have a part in this game.

"Real shit, it's okay if you not sure, K. Just know the opportunity is there if you want it." He didn't have to explain his reasoning to me.

"'Preciate that, my nigga. Just let me think on it," he said as I caught his eyes wander to something—his girl, Jai.

"No doubt."

"You better go get you a plate while you playing, Ty. You know how many greedy mothafuckas showed up?" he said, changing the subject.

"Man, you shole right. I'ma be mad as hell if all the macaroni gone."

"Shit, do you, nigga. We gon' chop it up later before you get outta here."

"Bet," I said, dapping him up while I went to go make my plate.

Little did I know, a plate wouldn't be the only thing I found my way to.

# *Ivy*

"Aniya, why you dressed like you on vacation or something? You ain't nowhere but in yo' cousin backyard." Sammy joked on Aniya as she smacked her lips.

"Whatever, hater. Don't be mad because I'm fine as fuck," she said, doing her model walk while I gassed her up.

"Don't nobody wanna see them ant bites you got. Sit yo' ass down," Sammy said while she started to hit him repeatedly.

"Ant bites my ass. My man loves everything about me. You just always hating."

He laughed. "Alright, Ni. When I throw yo' little ass in that pool, don't say nothing. You better make sure that's that good, expensive weave 'cause it's gon' be over for you."

"Nigga, I only rock the good, expensive kind. Thank you very much," Aniya said, swinging the twenty-six inches of Brazilian deep wave hair she had in her head.

"Y'all are really too much," I said, looking around. I was mainly keeping an eye out for my baby. He was in the pool with some other kids, having the time of his life. He was going to sleep so good tonight, and I was glad. Kacey liked to play grown and stay up all night. That only worked with his daddy, not me.

"Not they shooting dice over there." Aniya slightly laughed while we all turned our head the same way.

"See, I told y'all it was gon' be ghetto. Watch somebody start fighting when they lose they money," Sammy said, and we all laughed.

"Ni, how's school?" I asked her, moving on to something else.

"School just started, Ivy." She rolled her eyes playfully. "But I'm ready to get up out of there. This is my last year, thank God." Aniya was the baby of the family on both sides for me. She was the only person out of all of us who actually went to college. I knew for a fact I couldn't do it, but I was proud she was on the right path on walking across that stage. Her major was fashion, and her minor was business, so there was no doubt she would land on her feet after college.

Really, she was already doing her thing. She had a huge following on Instagram and Twitter. Many brands would pay her to promote their products. She even had a few endorsement deals. It was honestly dope to watch. I was proud of my baby cousin. At twenty-one, she was on her shit.

"Well, I'm proud of you. Keep doing what you're doing."

"Nah, we all proud of you. College is a big thing. Sometimes I wish I went," Sammy said.

"You can always go back," Aniya spoke up.

"For what? I already got my business going up. Ain't shit them people can teach me," Sammy said, talking his shit.

"You never know. Maybe they could offer you a class on how to stop being so fuckin' annoying." Aniya laughed and gave me a high five.

"Oh you talking shit? Bet," Sammy said. Hopping up and grabbing her by her legs.

"Sammy, no! Stop." Aniya kicked, and this time, he picked her up. She tried to put up a fight, but Sammy was just stronger.

At least she didn't go in by herself. She dragged him right in the water with her. I was damn near in tears. I always was whenever shit like this happened. Sammy loved to pick with us, and he always got under our skin. Luckily, we were with the shits. We stayed play fighting and joking on each other.

"What you over here drinking?" Rashad said, coming out of nowhere. I watched him take the seat next to me on the long pool chair with a red plastic cup in his hand just like me.

"Just a margarita. When did you get here?" I didn't even think he was coming to Kordell's welcome home party. They knew each other because of me and Jai, but still, they weren't really close.

"Maybe ten minutes ago."

"You see Kordell?"

"Yeah. We spoke for a minute. I'm glad he home, but really, I was looking for you," he said while I looked at Kacey and then him.

"For what?"

"Where Kacey at?" he said, ignoring my question.

"Over there in the pool," I said, pointing him out.

"How long y'all staying here?" he said, pulling out his phone and checking the time.

"I don't know. Why?"

"Because I needa keep tabs on my family, that's why. I heard about you and that nigga choppin' it up at the barbershop," he said while I rolled my eyes. I didn't know how he knew about the conversation with me and Q from earlier, but people were messy. There were plenty of people outside. Marie Cutz was in the heart of the hood. All the niggas kicked it in that area.

"Okay," I simply stated. The last thing I was about to do was cause a scene in front of all my family. I could've explained myself, but Rashad was only going to flip some shit on me and make me feel like I was wrong, like he always did. He could fuck multiple bitches, and it was cool, but if I even had an innocent conversation with a man, it was a problem.

Plus, he stayed trying to control me with money.

"Okay? Ivy, stop fuckin' playing with me. You want a nigga to get on yo' ass, I see. Always doing some dumb ass shit and wanna play innocent. You know what the fuck you be doing," he said.

I laughed to keep from cursing him out. "Shut the fuck up, Rashad. Damn, you always trip on me for the littlest shit ever. It wasn't nothing with me and Q. Besides, I'm single anyways." It seemed like he kept forgetting that shit, and it irritated the fuck out of me.

"You single, but still fuckin' me. You my business for life. Fuck is you saying, girl?" he said, raising his voice a little bit.

"I haven't fucked you in three months. Don't get me confused with them other bitches. If it's not about Kacey, then don't question me, simple," I said, snatching away from him since he wanted to grab my arm.

"Nah, you not finna be out here making me look bad just because you wanna be on ho shit."

"Rashad, please," I said, stopping myself before I could pop off. "Don't piss me off for real. I'm not about to do this with you. Leave me alone."

"I'm cool on yo' ass, Ivy. For real. You gon' need me before I need you, and that's a fact. Me and my son leaving.

Don't hit me to get him unless you can get yo' shit together, real talk," he said, getting up and going to get Kacey. Of course, his stupid ass wanted to bring our son into it. That was all he ever did when he was mad, and then when I would call, he wouldn't answer. He'd try to keep Kacey away from me for weeks if he could just because he felt a way toward me.

Well, I wasn't dealing with his shit not today.

Jumping up, I followed him to the pool. Sammy saw us from a distance, so immediately, he was on go behind me.

"Come on Kacey. You finna leave with daddy," Rashad called out to Kacey while he happily got out the pool.

"Kacey, you don't have to go if you don't want to. If you wanna play with your cousins, you can, and then later, you can see your dad," I told him.

"I wanna go with him, Mommy," Kacey said while I picked him up.

"Yeah, so let my son come with me, Ivy. Don't be on no extra shit," Rashad said while I looked at Kacey and then back at him.

"No," I politely told Rashad.

"No? Ivy, you got me fucked up," Rashad spat with rage.

"Nah, you got her fucked up, nigga. You got too much hostility going on to be around my cousin and her son. What's really going on?" Sammy said, now standing on my side.

"That's my fuckin' son too. You better gon' on with that bullshit. This ain't got shit to do with you. That's what the fuck going on," Rashad barked, approaching Sammy.

"What you tryna do?" Sammy moved me out the way, making me damn near fall.

"It's whatever with me," Rashad said, about to take off his jewelry.

"Stop. Don't do this in front of Kacey," I said, pushing Rashad back. "I got it, Sammy." I said, grabbing Rashad's arm as we walked to the front of the house. There were so many eyes on us and damn near all my family was on go. It was best if I got Rashad out of here quick. It was so selfish of us to be doing this on Kordell's day.

"Yo' cousin know he gotta see me for that weak ass shit. I know where to find him. Believe that," Rashad said, still upset.

I shook my head. "Rashad, just go. You can take Kacey with you. Just don't be on your petty shit when I call you," I said, about to hand Kacey over until all hell broke loose.

"Bitch ass nigga! What's up? You got something to say to my family? Say that shit to me!" I heard somebody yell. In the blink of an eye, almost all the men from the party were outside ready to fight my child's father.

"Shit, what's up?" Rashad said, clearly not backing down. Just like my family, he wanted all the smoke.

"Mommy, I'm scared." Kacey started to cry on my shoulder.

"Rashad, please," I begged, grabbing his shoulder.

"Nah, fuck that. These mothafuckas don't put fear in my heart. I'm with whatever," he said, pushing me back and almost making me and Kacey fall.

"Fuck," I said, putting Kacey down.

"No, Mommy! No," Kacey cried.

"Rashad, your son is scared! Stop!" I yelled out to him, but it was no use. By this time, a whole fight had broken out, and there wasn't nothing I could do.

My child's father was dead ass fighting my family right in front of his son. It was so hard to break him and Sammy up. They were at it for a good ten minutes strong, fighting from the parking lot all the way to the streets. This was a white neighborhood, so I was sure the laws would be called. They both knew how to handle themselves, so I could only imagine the damage.

"Ho ass nigga, I'll put you under! You lucky you my little cousin's pops, pussy!" Sammy yelled while Kordell held him back. He was the one to successfully break the two of them up.

"Aye! I know where to find you, boy! On my son, this shit ain't over! I got something for you, fuck nigga!" Rashad said with blood leaking from the side of his head.

It took me the longest to get Rashad to leave, and right before he did, he had to talk his shit to me. It was only right.

"This how you moving, Ivy? Bet. I'm done being nice. I know what it is, and I meant what I said. Yo' cousin got something coming… all of them niggas," he said, opening up his car door.

"What are you talking about? I didn't want this to happen. I tried to stop it."

"It's yo' fault shit even went left, but fuck it. Acting like I can't take my son. That's my fuckin' son too!" he yelled in my face. "Every time I see, them niggas it's up. You know what I'm on. And I'ma get my son later on, and I don't wanna hear shit from you. I'm cool on you, Ivy," he said, jumping in his car and speeding off.

I was so over this shit. I wanted to cry. In fact, I did. I felt crazy, having a mental breakdown with no shoes on in the middle of the damn street. I felt so bad inside that this happened, even though it wasn't on me. It killed me mainly because I knew Kacey was going to suffer someway, somehow because of Rashad and his childish ways. I just knew this day couldn't get any worse than what it already was.

"Ivy, there's nothing you can do now," Jai said, coming to get me.

"I just feel like breaking down. I can't win for fuckin' losing," I cried, feeling fucking defeated. So many things were going through my head right now, and I was letting all the bad thoughts eat me alive.

"I know. I know," she said, trying to soothe me.

"Where's Kacey?" I lifted my head from her shoulder.

"With Kordell. I can't believe Rashad did all that in front of his son," she said, taking my hand as we walked back to the driveway.

"Jai, I tried to stop it. Him and Sammy were both in the wrong. Even I feel responsible," I said, and she jumped in front of me.

"For what? You can't control them niggas acting like a pack of wild animals. Men and their egos." She laughed. "That wasn't on you. I don't care what you say."

I remained silent and walked inside of Jai and Kordell's crib. "You good, family?" Kordell said, approaching me with Kacey in his arms.

"Yeah, I—"

"What's wrong?" he said, looking at me and then in the directions of my eyes.

It was him, the man I thought I would never have to

cross paths with again, Ty.

He and Breeze were laughing about something, but once he laid eyes on me, his whole face got serious.

"Ivy," Kordell called my name.

"Huh? Umm... I'll take Kacey. We're about to go. Thank you for looking after him. I'm sorry this happened at your party," I said, taking Kacey from him. The whole time, Ty watched me intensively. He was shocked just like me. I saw it his eyes.

I didn't have anything to say to him. I tried to forget that night so badly, and I would've if it weren't for him showing up. I mean, why was he even here? Was this nigga stalking me? I knew he was crazy.

"You good, Ivy. You know we got you on this side."

"Ivy, you don't have to go. You and Kacey can spend the night," Jai said from behind me.

"No—"

"Aye, ain't you the bottle girl from the club. Aniya cousin. Small world," Breeze said, noticing me.

All eyes were on me at this point, including Ty's, and it felt weird. Without saying another word, I went to get my purse and car keys so Kacey and I could leave.

"Did I say something wrong?" I heard Breeze say from afar.

I was in one of those moods where I wanted to tune the whole world out, so I left. I wasn't in the mood to be around my mother either. That was why I made sure I got some of our clothes from Jai's and got us a hotel room for the night.

Watching Kacey sleep brought me a peace of mind. As soon as we got here, we ordered room service, watched TV, and I put him in the bath. At least, he enjoyed himself today.

I called Rashad at least twenty times, and each call was forwarded to his voicemail.

Looking at the digital clock on the nightstand, the time read 11:18 p.m.

I was just about to go to sleep myself when I got a notification on my phone.

Watching the unsaved number pop up on my screen, a sense of confusion washed over my face.

*(786) 631-4713: We gotta talk. Hit me back. Ty*

# Jainice

"All this for your man?" Kordell's deep voice boomed through the kitchen. There he stood, shirtless in a pair of gray sweatpants on and a fresh line up. That was all I needed to see to get excited between my legs. He never had to do too much. He was just naturally fine, and the slightest things made me want to feel him inside of me.

It blew my mind how he came home with more tattoos than when he left, especially on his chest. *Only God Can Judge Me* was written in cursive from shoulder to shoulder, and he even got my name on his arm. I thought it was cute. The day he got it, he called me up and let me know. I wasn't really surprised, because in prison, you had nothing but time on your hands, which meant you got creative and did things people wouldn't expect.

"Of course, daddy." I smiled, looking back at him. I woke up at seven this morning and decided to cook a big breakfast for my man—eggs, bacon, sausage, grits, blueberry muffins and pancakes. Usually, I would have never been up this early, but since Kordell had been home, it was like I was on his schedule. We did everything together from waking up to going to sleep, and I wasn't complaining about it one bit. I missed him way too much for all of that.

Picking me up, he kissed my lips twice. "I love you, Jai, so fuckin' much. I can never repay you for all of the shit you did for me. Half of the shit, I didn't even tell you to do. You just did it."

Away or in my presence, Kordell would forever express his gratitude toward me. He wasn't one of those niggas who put up a front just because he was in jail, and I wasn't one of those bitches holding a nigga down just for him to get out and dog me like I meant nothing. Nah, we were better than that. His sentencing was a hurdle, but it wasn't our first. We'd been through so many things together, however, this obstacle like many before made us stronger.

I could never get tired of hearing the love of my life thank me for what I'd done for him, but I was at the point in my life where I needed no validation at all. We both knew what was up. We were locked in for about seven years. Where the fuck was I going? Where the fuck was he going?

"You don't ever get tired of thanking me?" I joked while he stepped back and bit his lip. "Never." He smiled, making me do the same.

"I'm just playing, baby, but you're welcome. I'm glad you're home," I said, reaching my arms out, so that he could fill them with his warm embrace.

No exaggeration, I probably hugged this man damn

near a thousand times since he'd been home. It still felt like a dream to me. Through it all, I never lost faith when it came to him. So many people around me said that I was crazy. They said he would never come home, but here he was. His tight grip around my waist was proof enough for me. I didn't care what anybody had to say. Kordell was for me. He was my person.

Hearing a few sniffles from me, Kordell pulled away from me and spoke. "You crying again? You know I don't like it when you cry."

Kordell always told me my tears were like kryptonite. They were his weakness, and whenever he even saw water form in my eyes, it did something to him. But these were tears of joys. For the first time in five years, I was genuinely happy again. Some may say it was the hardest thing in the world to get that happiness back you longed for, but I'd beg to differ. Shit, I was so happy that it scared me inside. Thinking about all the what-ifs fucked with my mental.

"These are happy tears, K." I assured him.

Staring deeply in my eyes, he sighed. "You sure, Jai? Because sometimes it's hard for me to tell with you," he said, surprising me a bit.

"What do you mean?" Confused, I got off the countertop and started making the eggs. Everything else was basically done.

Following my every step, Kordell was right behind me. "The eggs can wait," he said, grabbing my hand from behind me. "We gotta talk, Jai," he said while I sighed and turned around to face him.

"What's up?"

"That's what I'm tryna see. I may have been gone for a minute, but I can always tell when something is not right with you." That was nothing but the truth.

I couldn't keep anything from K, even if I tried, which was why the topic of birth control had been so dreading to me. It wasn't like I didn't want to tell him. I just didn't know how. I didn't even have the decency to inform him that I was getting on. Sure, it was my body and my choice, but he and I were a team. And I did regret it.

I was just scared. Not of long-term commitment though, I actually wanted that, but being a baby mama with nothing to show for? Kordell could've easily persuaded me not to get on birth control and then gotten me pregnant. I wasn't trying to risk that. Marriage was a bigger priority than a kid, and if he couldn't understand that, I'm sorry.

"I-I-I don't know…"

"Say what's on your mind, Jai." Kordell interrupted me.

"Can we just eat?" I said, attempting to bypass him, but he grabbed my arm and pulled me back in front of him. I tried my hardest not to look in those eyes of his because I would feel nothing but guilt deep inside. I couldn't lie to him ever, so the truth would be out within seconds.

"When I first got out, what was the first thing I asked you?" he said, placing his finger to my chin and lifting it so that I was now looking at him.

"You asked me was there anything I wanted to know in regards of you and us," I stated.

"And what did you say?"

"I said there was nothing I wanted to know."

"Exactly, Jai. You said that shit out yo' own mouth. You telling me you lying to me now? That's what the fuck we on?" he said in disbelief.

I got it. This wasn't like me at all. We always kept it real with each other. It was just the way I was feeling that couldn't be expressed. It was weird, and I didn't know what to call it.

"I would never lie to you, Kordell. I'm just scared."

"Of what?" he said, backing me against the counter. Irritation was written all over his face. It was like I was annoying him with the way I was acting, and shit, him being annoyed because of my annoyance was annoying me.

"Scared that I would lose you again. Scared that I might have to hold things down on my own. Scared that things between us won't evolve the way I want them to," I confessed while he took a step back and scratched his chin.

"You serious?"

"I am."

The whole time Kordell was gone, he never mentioned marrying me once. It was strange because from all the emails and phone calls that were being held between the two of us, anyone would've thought marriage came up. Five years away from your girl is a long time. Why wouldn't anyone want to discuss a future with the love of their life? In my eyes, if they could mention kids, they could mention marriage, period. I wanted more, and if he loved me like he said he did, then he'd give it to me. No questions asked.

"Kordell, you don't know what it was like for me outside. Just like you were in there struggling, so was I. I spent so many sleepless nights, up thinking about you. If it wasn't my anxiety, it was my depression. I love you, but this time, things have to be right. No mistakes," I spoke.

He put his head down and laughed some. "Fuck, Jai, if you wanna know if I'm going back to hustling, then just say that shit. What you over here sugarcoating shit for, girl?" he yelled, taking me back some.

"Huh? I shouldn't have to ask you that question. It shouldn't even be a thought. You should want better for yourself after five years of being away from your girl and your family."

I'd be honest and say the question of if Kordell was going back to his old ways had popped in my head countless times, but I shouldn't have to ask him, because that was on him. He was a grown ass man, which meant he was in control of his own actions. It wasn't like I was going to leave him if he said yes to hustling again, but I just expected different. He never gave me the impression that he would leave his old life behind him, but at the same time, he didn't say he wouldn't. I guess I just assumed.

"So you tryna change a nigga now? Is that what it is?" he said with a raised eyebrow, and I rolled my eyes.

"I would never. I knew the type of nigga you was before I got with you, and I was cool with it. All I'm saying is there's more to life than being in the streets. I mean, don't you want more? More with me? I just wanna be happy with you with no worries, K."

Expressing my feelings was something I struggled with sometimes. In the beginning, I would hold things back from Kordell because I didn't want to come off as the type of girl who was always complaining or couldn't handle a certain lifestyle. Now I'd grown as a woman and realized what I really wanted. I figured if I couldn't be vulnerable with my significant other, than what was the point in even being together? Being a woman, myself, I thought it was important for women to differentiate from the things they were with and what weren't with.

Not saying that Kordell had ever tried me on some weak shit, but still, it was important to me to have a voice and say-so in this relationship.

"Well, if you would've asked me, you would've known that I wasn't on that anymore." He didn't mean that last statement. He couldn't have. I just knew.

He couldn't even answer the one simple question that I asked him.

"If I ask you to believe in me, would that be too much to ask for, Jai? You supposed to be my girl."

Quickly defending that title, I spoke up. "I am your girl, and I do believe in you."

"The fuck you over here harboring thoughts and feelings for then? I ain't never made it seem like you couldn't come to me about anything. Stop moving weird. I ain't fuckin' with it," he said while I crossed my arms and smacked my lips.

"Nigga what? You gon' really fix your lips to say some shit like that? Move," I said, pushing him out of the way, leaving the kitchen.

As long as he knew me, I'd never moved funny. What the fuck was Kordell talking about? He could miss me with the bullshit. I could tell him that much.

Sitting on the living room couch, I turned the TV on full blast. Fuck it. I felt like being petty. Kordell called my name countless times, but this was my way of blocking his ass out.

"Why you choose this morning to show the fuck out?" he said, snatching the remote out of my hands and tossing it to the ground.

"I don't know. Why you choose this morning to get on my damn nerves?" I replied.

He sucked his teeth. "Watch out, Jai," he said, shooting me a serious look.

I wasn't even the disrespectful type. I was just annoyed.

I wasn't in the mood to be going back and forth with Kordell. He could do whatever he wanted to because I was over it. Attempting to get up, I was pushed right back on the couch.

"Come on, man, and make these eggs. I'm hungry as fuck."

"Nigga, fuckin' starve for all I care," I mumbled to

myself, trying to get up again, but the same thing occurred.

"What?" he said, quickly cocking his head in my direction and grabbing both of my legs. "Wanna repeat that shit?" he said, staring back at me with a "try me" expression.

I remained silent and exhaled dramatically.

"Thought so."

Pushing me back gently, he moved in between my legs and undid my robe. Underneath it, I wore a Savage X Fenty matching pink lace set. Eyeing from my breasts to my thick thighs, he was mesmerized. When Kordell was locked up, I made sure to keep my body nice and tight, whether I was working out, doing body sculpting, or simply dieting. My ass was homegrown, and that seemed to be what he loved the most about me. However, I did get my breasts done twice, but that didn't make a difference, because I was a bad bitch either way.

"When I'm done fuckin' you, I want my eggs scrambled with cheese," he said, sliding his hand down to my jewel while he massaged it softly in a circular motion.

"Umm, I didn't say I wanted to fuck you."

Kordell smirked and then licked his lips. "You always wanna fuck me, baby."

I couldn't even keep a straight face. I could never stay mad at him. We were just a goofy ass couple who loved to fuck all the time.

Before I could say another word, his lips crashed into mine, making me forget I was even mad at him. K was a hood ass nigga, but when he kissed me with those soft lips and showed me the affection that I loved so much, I could only see him as being my lover—nothing more, nothing less. I didn't even know why I acted like I didn't want to fuck him, because I always did, just like he said. I craved that man.

Feeling his fingers creep into my thong, I was ready and willing to feel the pleasure he was about to give me. Once he stuck his fingers inside of me, I moaned, giving him more access into my mouth. The more he moved in and out of me, the wetter I got. Clenching my thighs, ready to cum, K picked me up from the couch and put me against the wall.

He moved my body further up onto the wall until he was leveled with my pussy. With no warning, he started to eat me like he hadn't ate for days. Just last night, his face was in the same place, but each time he ate me, he made that shit count. That was what I loved.

K gave me eye contact, but it didn't last that long, because his concentration was on my pussy. "Shit, K," I moaned, allowing my eyes to roll in the back of my head. I was so close to cumming, and he knew. Five years away, and he still knew my body and what to do with it. *Talk about a man.* "Oh, fuck!" I cried, trying to push his head back some.

He nearly broke my finger. There wasn't no running from him. I should've known. Within seconds, I was dripping all over him. He licked me with pride.

When he put me down from wall, I nearly fell on my ass. When Kordell peeped my knees buckle, he let out a laugh and then picked me up. I grabbed the back of his neck, and just like before, our tongues were connected. The taste of me only turned me on more.

Kordell sat us on the couch, and I reached for the band of his sweatpants. Once my hand found his hard dick, I started to stroke him a few times, making him bite his lip. I got off of him, never letting go of his dick until I was ready to suck it. Once I did, there was no complaints from him, just like there was none from me.

Stroking him with two hands, I ran my tongue up and down and then went in for the kill. By this time, he was fully hard, allowing my saliva and good throat take control of him.

"Damn, Jai. I'm in heaven," he moaned while he pulled my hair and guided my head up and down on his dick. The feeling of sucking him up made me feel so good because I knew any time my mouth touched him, he enjoyed it.

Pulling my head up, he lifted me directly on his dick. That shit gave me chills, making me instantly moan. Kordell grabbed my hips and started to guide me up and down on him until I started to fuck him back. Undoing my bra, he kissed and sucked on each of my breasts, making sure he left his mark. Next was my neck.

He flipped me over, put my legs into the air, and starting to drill me. These were those long and hard strokes, the type that'd get me pregnant if I weren't careful.

"Kordell, don't stop fucking me," I screamed, feeling my walls starting to tighten up.

"Fuck," he grunted, pulling me closer so I could feel everything he was offering me. "Not yet," he said, placing his hand on my left breast while he continued to give me those good strokes. He knew I was about to cum.

"I… mmmm," I moaned, not even able to finish my sentence. Feeling Kordell's warm semen fill me up, I started to feel guilt.

He thought we would be bringing a child into this world any day now. Truth be told, we wouldn't. Not until things were established, and we both could be honest with ourselves.

# *Ivy*

"I was wondering when you was gon' come up here and say something to me, Ivy Marie," my grandpa Leon said while he stood in the kitchen, fixing himself a sandwich. It was the longest I hadn't spoken to him face-to-face. It definitely wasn't intentional. It was just things were still rocky between me and my mother. She wasn't going to apologize, and I didn't feel like going to jail for putting hands on her, so it was best for me to keep my distance.

I would say, living out of a hotel for these past couple of days hadn't been all of that. Sure, we had a pool, room service, and even a comfortable robe, but it wasn't home. I still got that lonely feeling at night, even with Kacey wrapped up in my arms those late nights. We needed something for us, but I couldn't leave my grandpa's just yet. It just didn't feel right.

Standing in front of me was my handsome grandpa. His skin was smooth and chocolate, and he wore a pair of jeans with a blue button-down shirt. On his feet, he wore his favorite brown boots. They were so old, but he managed to keep them up to par. My grandpa was a hardworking man since the age of ten. He kept a job, whether it was mowing the lawn or carrying groceries. He stayed active and making money. That was the way he always was.

Just like with Grandma Marie, I was close with Grandpa Leon. I didn't have the typical relationship with my parents like others did. My mother was always angry or either depressed for as long as I could remember, and my father was nowhere to be found. Truth was, he could walk right past me, and I wouldn't even know who he was. It'd been that way since birth in my eyes.

Just because my parents couldn't be the parents I needed them to be didn't mean I would follow in their footsteps. Together or apart, Rashad and I would be the best parents we could be for Kacey. I did want my son to experience a two-parent household just because I didn't experience it. Quiet as it was kept, that was why I stayed with Rashad after the things he would put me through. I should've been left that situation alone, but only I know when I was done with a nigga. I mean, he was my child's father.

"I'm sorry, Grandpa. I did miss you. Did you get the money I sent you through Jai?" I asked while he bit into his sandwich and made a face.

I noticed he managed to cut the crust off his bread. Kacey was the exact same way. My son was such a picky eater at only three years old. I would think he would like everything, but there were so many different foods that he didn't like.

Wiping his hands together, he shook his head. "I don't

need no money from you. I just wanted to see you and my boy. I gave that money right back to Jainice. You know better than that." He chuckled while he took another bite of his sandwich.

My grandpa wasn't a fan of random gifts. The only time he let his grandkids spoil him was during the holidays and his birthday. It was kind of frustrating because all we wanted to do was shower him with love like he did for us all these years, but his pride wouldn't allow it. He always said he didn't need materialistic things, just us.

It was because of him that we were all so family oriented. I took that to the heart. I didn't play about my family at all. They meant too much to me, even my mother. No matter what she said or did to me, my love for her was always present. Call me crazy, but I yearned for my mother's love, and one day I would get it.

I sighed and laughed some. "Sorry."

"Mhm, where is Kacey?" he asked, grabbing his plate while I followed him into the living room. The television was the first thing that caught my eye. I let another laugh out when I realized the small box TV had been replaced with a sixty-inch television with a matching stand. This had Sammy written all over it.

My grandpa was so old-school. He didn't care for the latest technology or upscale décor. He would settle for what he had. My mother and I both had to beg him to let us change some things around the house. It was like pulling teeth, but he let us redo everything except the kitchen and his room.

I understood it though. His heart was set on the way things had been for the last fifteen years or so. The house was in the family for the longest, and he was holding on to the idea of keeping things the same. Grandma Marie was gone, and he needed those memories. We all did.

"Sammy been here, huh?" I shook my head while we both sat on the brown plush couch. The whole living room was decorated in that color to be exact. He said it gave him that homey feeling, that along with all the childhood pictures of his grandkids and kids.

"Boy came over here six in the damn morning tryna mount a damn television. I don't know what's wrong with him," he said, and I cracked up.

"It is nice though. You get way more channels and better quality."

"I don't care about that. Long as I get to watch the news, *CSI*, and my Tyler Perry plays, I was good to go."

"I'm already knowing, Grandpa," I said, leaning my head back so that it rested on the pillow.

"So what your mama do to piss you off?" he spoke, making me open my eyes.

"What she always does." I shrugged.

"I don't know why she act like that. Ever since your daddy left after she had you, she ain't been right. I knew that man was the devil in disguise. No good." My grandpa sucked his teeth. "Do me a favor and grab me a water bottle out the fridge, Marie." Sometimes he would call me by my middle name, which was my grandma's first name. I thought it was sweet. We all had some of her inside of us.

Hopping up, I went to the refrigerator and did like he asked. I noticed that the refrigerator was damn near empty. Usually, I would do the grocery shopping, but my mother said she'd go this time. I even gave her $300 to make sure she got everything she needed. We didn't cook as much as we did when Grandma Marie was here, but we still ate. There should be way more food in this damn refrigerator. Even the cabinets were damn near empty.

"Grandpa Leon, my mother didn't go to the grocery store?" I asked him while I handed him the water bottle.

He opened it and took a long sip, draining the water to the middle of the bottle and then spoke. "Marie, I don't know. There's plenty of food in there."

I noticed my grandpa was always the peacemaker. He never wanted drama, especially between his family, hence, why he was trying to cover for his daughter because there was clearly nothing in that kitchen. I didn't know where the money went, but next time I would be doing the grocery shopping.

"You need something from the store? I can go there before I have to go to work. Just write me a list," I told him while he finished his sandwich up.

"No."

"Okay, well, I'll still get a few things for you. Milk, eggs, bread, water you know?" I said while he looked over to me.

"Sure, thing baby. Where's Kacey at?" he asked again, changing the subject.

"With his dad. He's watching him since I have to work tonight. I'll bring him by tomorrow after school."

Getting in contact with Rashad was a hassle. He was still in his feelings about what went down at Kordell's welcome home party and blamed me. Apparently, it was on me because it was my family, but whatever. I wasn't thinking about that ghetto ass shit anymore, and neither should he. Niggas always had to take shit personal when it came to beef and all of that just because nobody wanted to seem weak. It was stupid to me, but I wouldn't speak on it.

Kacey was with his father, happy. That was good enough for me, regardless if Rashad was still salty or not. It wasn't about us.

"Okay, sounds good to me. I miss my boy," he said, grabbing the remote from the table and starting to flip through the channels.

"He misses you too, trust."

My grandpa and Kacey's relationship was so beautiful. They were stuck like glue. Grandpa Leon made sure to spend as much quality time with Kacey as possible. I mean, he was his only great-grandbaby for now. They did everything together. Kacey enjoyed the time they spent with each other, whether it was fishing or simply taking a car ride. I absolutely loved it.

"What you tryna watch, Grandpa?" I asked, watching him struggle through the guide.

Sammy probably set up this TV and didn't tell him which channels were which or how to work the remote. My grandpa was in his seventies, so of course he wasn't going to know everything about his upgrade.

"I'm tryna watch OWN," he said, handing me the remote.

"Let me find it… there." Clicking on the channel, I put the remote down and put my attention on the TV.

"How was your day today, Grandpa?"

"Good. I'm still here. I went over to that soul food restaurant and picked me up a good ole plate. They got some good fried chicken, but it ain't better than your grandma's. I tell you that much." "Nobody can cook better than Grandma Marie." She taught me everything I know in the kitchen, me and Jai both. We'd all been cooking since kids. I enjoyed being in the kitchen, even if it wasn't the same. I didn't think there was anything I couldn't make.

"Ha, you got that right. Baby, go grab your grandpa a blanket from out the closet upstairs. It's cold." He yawned.

I knew, soon, he would be out for a nap. Anytime he slept, I didn't bother him one bit. He was the type to move around all day. Whether it was visiting family or at church, my grandpa was always on the go. He needed that sleep, and I wanted him to have it.

"Okay, I'll be right back." Getting up, I lowered the volume on the TV and went upstairs. I hadn't been here in a minute, but as soon as I saw my room, all I wanted to do was get inside my bed. That would have to wait until tonight though.

I was torn at first about being around my mother, but looking around upstairs, I knew I had to come back home. The floors were dusty, the upstairs plants hadn't been watered, nor were there clean towels. I just couldn't understand why things were so out of place around here. I hadn't been gone for that long.

I mean, my mother wasn't working, so she had all the time in the world to keep things together. Her reason for staying home was she needed to look after my grandpa. True, he lived alone for a while after the passing of his wife, but I was well aware that he could take care of hisself. She knew that too. She just wanted an excuse to quit her job and live rent free. Everything was paid off over here. So it was like yeah, she cared for her father, but at the same time, she needed a stable place to stay at. A place she had nothing to worry about but a bottle from time to time.

Shit was sad, but she was who she was. We just had to accept it or keep our distance as long as we could. It was hard living under a roof with her because she felt like she called the shots around here. She acted like it was a problem that I came to stay with my grandpa. Lord knows we had plenty of space, but even if we had a hundred rooms, my presence would still get under her skin.

Life like as a teen sucked. I got out of there at seventeen and didn't look back not one time. Who could blame me? Things were a lot way worse back then though. My mother would get so drunk every night that I would have to stay up and take care of her. Half of the time, I missed school, but I didn't give a fuck, because I hated it there anyways. I preferred to be somewhere, riding with the top down with Q, getting into shit I didn't need to be.

Point was I did everything I could to help her from covering for her to offering rehab, yet I got treated like a damn stepchild. I didn't get it. Why did she dislike me so much?

Opening the closet door, I grabbed a single blanket and shut the door back. I was just about to head back downstairs when I realized my mother's door was cracked open. Some might say if I had any sense, I wouldn't dare go in there, but right now, I only felt curiosity. I didn't know what was going on with my mother, but I was sure about to find out.

When I entered her room, I noticed it was just as dirty as the house. In fact, it was worse. The bed wasn't made, there were clothes all over the floor, and she managed to have plenty of snack wrappers and fast-food bags around. It was disgusting and disrespectful if you asked me. Never in a million years would Grandma Marie find this acceptable. She didn't play about the cleanliness of her home.

I could still smell that combination of Fabuloso, Pine-Sol, and carpet freshener that she would use each morning to clean the house. Grandma Marie knew just the right amount of bleach to wipe the counters down with so the smell wouldn't take over the entire house. I still remembered those times as a kid when my cousins and I would spend a night and she'd wake us up bright and early just to clean. Back then, I couldn't stand the idea of being woken up out my sleep just to clean with my grandma, but now, I'd do anything to be in that position again.

She didn't feel bad at all putting us to work. If anything, she drowned our complaining out with some Kirk Franklin and went about her day. The breakfast she made after that would make us forget even waking up so early. Sometimes she would cook before just to butter us up. I missed those pancakes of hers. Each time I'd ask her how'd she make them so good, she would tell me *baby, everything I make, I make with love.*

That had to be it because I was good at pancakes, but they never tasted as good as hers. Maybe that was what I was missing, love.

Walking over to the bed, I picked up a notepad that was filled with at least ten to twenty phone numbers written in it. Some were highlighted and others were crossed out with a red pen. None of the numbers looked familiar to me, yet I still scanned over them, hoping that I would be able to uncover something.

Flipping through the pages, there were a list of initials, and just like the numbers, they were highlighted. I couldn't take a minute trying to figure out what they meant this time because my mother was home. Hearing her voice from downstairs scared the fuck outta me. She would throw a whole fit if she knew I was in her room.

Still, I needed to know the truth, no matter how bad it was, so I ripped the page out, folded it up, and quickly stuffed it in my pocket. I almost broke my damn neck trying to hurry up and get out of her room. Thank God, I made it just in time, meeting her at the stairs.

"What are you doing here?" she asked with a smug look on her face. She didn't need to tell me she didn't want me here, because her face already let me know that.

"I came to see Grandpa. He wanted me to bring him a blanket from upstairs," I said, looking at the blanket in my hand stupidly and then back at her.

"Mhm, gone on. I'm tired and need to lay down," she said, pushing me to the side.

That was when I noticed her freshly manicured nails and the few shopping bags she was carrying. Hell, she'd even got her hair trimmed into a middle-part bob. She obviously had the funds to do what she wanted to do, so why not put food in the house for her father? She was going to make a way for herself, but how about her dad?

"Why didn't you go grocery shopping for the house like you said you were? I gave you money and everything, Ma. You're supposed to be looking out for Grandpa," I blurted out.

I instantly regretted doing that when I saw the look in her eyes. They were filled with rage, and I had only asked her one simple question.

"Excuse me? Ivy, don't you ever fucking question me about what I do for my father like I haven't been taking care of him. Remember, it's me cooking, cleaning, and tending to him while you're busy chasing after niggas and fucking for change. It's clear I'm the only one who cares for him. So if you're gonna be here, at least shut the fuck up and stay out of my way. Understood?" she said, pointing her finger in my face.

"If you call yourself taking care of him, then you're doing a terrible job, Ma. The floors are dusty, and there's no food in the refrigerator. Shall I proceed? You know I do everything I can to help out around here. There's no need to speak on me like you know my life," I let it be known. I was more than helpful around here, even when I didn't stay here. I was just the type of person to make sure my family was good at all times, whether they needed me or not. My mother knew that well enough because even when she did me dirty, I was always there to put money in her pocket.

She cocked her head to the side and stepped back some like what I said was so bad. Nah. It was just the truth.

"I know all about your fucked up life!" She spat and

shook her head. "Chile, you better gone on. I'm not gon' tell you again," she said, running her fingers through her hair.

"You don't. You're too focused on the old me that you won't allow yourself to get in touch with the new me. If only you would try, you'd see I'm different. Things are different."

"The hell if you are," she said, becoming defensive once again. "You're the same ole spoiled ass little girl that you've always been. Depending on others like you're not supposed to hold your own. You're weak and needy, and you know it. Don't you dare come up in here trying to judge me like you're better than me. You're just like me!" she spat while she grabbed my arm forcefully.

"I'm not! I could never be!" I yelled as a single tear escaped my eye. That was what I feared the most in this fucked-up life—that I would be just like my mother in the end, bitter, mean, and angry inside with no love. I tried my hardest to steer away from the things she would do and say. I had to be better than her, not just as a mother, but overall as a human being. There's no telling what would happen to me if I allowed my heart to be filled with so much malice.

"You are!" she shouted as she grabbed my head with both hands and brought my face to hers. "Don't you see yourself when you look into my eyes? All I see is me when I look into yours," she whispered in a saddened tone, seeming breathless.

Each second I spent looking into her eyes, I did see something. I saw sorrow, hurt, confusion, and a tad bit of love, but no me. Until I left this earth, I would say I was nothing like my mother. I stood on that. Still, I wanted to be there for her and with her. In my heart, I felt like I could change her and help her become a better person. It wasn't too late for a mother-daughter relationship for me. Hopefully, I would have that mindset a little longer. Sometimes I grew tired to the point where I wanted to say fuck it.

"Hey, what's going on up there?" my grandpa said from the bottom of the stairs.

Hearing his voice made my mother snap out of her thoughts. She quickly let me go and then stared at me for a few seconds. "Just disappear again, Ivy. It was better that way." She wiped her tears before they could form and disappeared into her room.

Numerous times, I called for her, and never did she respond.

Taking a deep breath, I went back downstairs. "Got your blanket," I said, handing it to my grandpa, who still stood at the bottom of the steps.

"Look at me," he said, grabbing my chin.

I tried my hardest to avoid eye contact just like I

wanted to avoid this conversation that I was sure he wanted to have.

"What happened up there?"

So much sincerity was within him, but I just couldn't talk right now. "What always happens. Come on, let's go watch some TV," I said, leading the way to the couch, and he followed.

We sat there and watched a few episodes of *For Better or Worse*, and then I was out like a light, sleeping on my grandpa's shoulder. It felt so peaceful for that time being, but I could never stay too long.

I had to work.

*

"Ivy, what am I gonna do?" Jai complained to me while I sat passenger side in her 2020 Mercedes-AMG G63 G-Wagon. She was obsessed with the color burgundy, so it was only right she got her car in that color. The inside was just as nice with the heated leather seats and the LED lights. She even got her name written in the seats. Just like me, Jai enjoyed the finer things in life, it was the only way we knew.

"About what? And make it quick. You know Montell ass is gonna trip if I'm late again."

I couldn't believe this girl came all the way to my job just to vent—well, actually, I could because whenever Jai wanted to talk, she didn't waste any time. She didn't really have any girlfriends. Neither did I, so we confided in each other about everything. She knew my secrets, and I knew hers.

"I don't even know why you still working at this damn club. You should just find you a new hustle. Nails, lashes, clothes, or something," she said, and I rolled my eyes.

"If I would've knew this was gonna be your energy, I would've clocked the fuck in already. Hell, I would've stayed at Grandpa Leon's with my mother if I wanted to hear somebody down me."

"I'm not downing you. I would never. I'm just saying, there's something better out there for you." It was easy for her to say that because she didn't have to work. Not only was she with a nigga with a bag, but she never worked a nine-to-five ever. She was so popping that she got paid to host clubs or promote something, and that alone paid the bills.

It was different for me. I wasn't a broke bitch, but things were a little more complex for me. I had a child to look after. I couldn't waste time trying to get into something new. I was going to stick to what I knew. Besides, I was damn good at being a bottle girl. Sex truly sells, and I wasn't talking about actually fucking a nigga in here. My face, body, and popularity put money in my pockets.

It was easy for me. By now, I learned the game full

circle. I knew how to make more than what people expected me to make. Mainly because of rule number twelve: A good night is still a bad night. No matter how good of a night you're having, make them niggas think you didn't make shit. That way, they'd reach in their pockets and give you something extra. That worked every time, and I didn't feel bad about it, ever. It was either finesse or get finessed. A nigga wasn't about to run over me, period.

Going back to what was important, I spoke up. "Why did you come here, Jai? What's up?" I knew it was something about Kordell because what else was there to stress about with her? Only thing she had to do was tell me, and I was going to listen... only for a good eight minutes because I had to go.

"It's Kordell."

I gasped dramatically. "Really?"

"Fuck you." She threw up the middle finger, and I laughed.

"All I'm saying is I know you, cousin. What's the problem? You got about five minutes."

"I think Kordell is going back to the block, and I don't wanna be a dumb ho, waiting for him to fall, just to see him locked up again or dead just because I love him," she flat-out responded.

"Well damn, talk about transparency. If you could tell

me this, why can't you tell him the same thing?" I wondered.

"That's just it. I did, Ivy. We had a conversation this morning, more like an argument. I told him how I felt. He just thinks I have no faith in him like he's gonna fuck up again or something. I don't know." Jai shrugged while she pulled her hair to one side and looked over to me. "What should I do?"

"Trust your nigga."

Kordell never gave me the vibe of an ain't-shit ass nigga. He was solid in my eyes and just right for Jai. It honestly blew me how hard Jai was making things. I thought she should give him a chance to prove himself to her and not assume. After serving those five years, he should want to be on the same page as his girl. He knew Jai was one of a kind. It didn't get any better than her. Hopefully, for both of their sakes, they could get it together.

I wasn't an expert on relationships or anything, because I'd been through some shit myself—going back to a nigga countless times, letting shit slide, and acting like I didn't know what was really going on. Jai and Kordell were different from anything I'd ever experienced in my book. He never played her out and had always been him. That was why I was vouching for them as unit.

"How can I when he looked me in my eyes and lied to me? As soon as I asked him that question and he said no, I knew it was a lie. He might not have said yes just yet about going back to his old ways, but that nigga definitely has his toe in that water. It's only a matter of time before he takes that full dive in, Ivy."

"He won't." I thought out loud.

"You don't know him like I do. I didn't want to do this, but maybe I have to give him that ultimatum."

"Which is..." I trailed off.

"Me or the streets."

When I heard Jai say those words to me, I felt disbelief. Never had I thought it would come to this, and I was sure she didn't either. The crazy part is she was serious as a heart attack. One thing I learned about my cousin was when she said she was done with something, that was it. In the back of my mind, I thought Kordell would never be that stupid to choose that life over Jai, but when I looked at Jai, things were different. She thought otherwise.

Turning my whole body to her, I asked her this one question, "You think it'll come down to that? Honestly, Jai?"

"I don't know, but if it does, I have to be prepared for that."

I grabbed her hand. "Do you hear yourself? This is Kordell. You know you're his other half, bitch. You not going anywhere, and neither is he. I know it. All you need to do is have another conversation with him, one that doesn't end with fucking and sweeping shit under the rug, and then the two of you should be good.

She laughed and smacked her lips. "Now how do you know that's what happened?"

"Bitch, because I know you. Next time, hold off on that good cat until things get established."

She gave me a look. "Better said than done. I spent way too long not getting any dick. You really think I'm gon' pass up the opportunity on getting some?" she said, and we started to laugh.

"Hell nah."

"Exactly."

"Well, you needa figure out some things more than ever, since I'm sure you still haven't told Kordell that you're on birth control." I remembered.

Jai made a face and then rolled her eyes. "Have a nice shift, Ivy."

"Oh, I will. You know I got a thing for the bag," I said, opening up her car door. "Just know I'm serious."

"I know. Let's do lunch tomorrow or something. Okay?" she said, starting up her car.

"You know I love to eat. I'll be there." I smiled while she did the same.

"Greedy ass girl, bye."

"Bye." I grabbed my gym bag and closed her car door.

"Cutting it close there, aren't we?" Darren chuckled as I entered Club Wishes.

"Not close enough clearly."

"Tell that to Montell," he said, blowing smoke from his Black.

"I would prefer if his ass didn't say shit to me." Montell was a pure asshole, but he was very calculated when it came to his bread. I'd give him that. He even kept me working floor three, so my pockets were way fuller these days. However, I still didn't like him.

Darren shook his head and walked with me to the back where the dressing rooms were. "You have a good shift, Ivy."

"You too," I replied and entered inside.

Every shift was the same for me—long yet never boring. Since Club Wishes was the hottest club in Miami, people tended to come through the week and on weekends. Montell said there were no days off because a day off meant him missing out on money, and he wasn't having that. I worked four days a week, sometimes five when I was needed.

"Aye, y'all! Look who's back, my bitch Gabby!" Marissa shouted while all the ladies clapped like she was a damn celebrity or something. I, on the other hand, continued to lay my baby hairs in the mirror.

"That's right. I'm back and I'm better. I know bitches thought they could replace me, but they could never."

Looking in the mirror, I seen Gabby staring directly at me.

"Just ignore her ass, Ivy. Fuck her," I said to myself while I continued to get my hair together. Obviously, she heard I took over her spot on floor three and was in her feelings. If she wanted me to work floor two again, she would have to take that up with Montell because I wasn't going anywhere unless he said so. That bitch Gabby didn't put fear in my heart. None of these bitches did.

"Many *try* to be as bad as you, but they always fail," Marissa said, now looking directly at me. "Oh, I know that's right. Ivy, hear me loud and clear."

Once I heard my name, I dropped my edge brush and turned around.

"Your time working high stakes has came and left, baby girl. By time, I work my magic, you'll be long gone back to middleville, or worse, the bottom, where you truly belong." Gabby smirked.

"Or I'll stay right where I'm at and you downgrade. I must say, I don't know if the niggas down there make as much as the ones on floor three. So this time, you might have to come out of your own pocket to get rid of a pregnancy by a nigga who doesn't give a fuck about you. Isn't that what happened the last time and why you've been gone all this time?" I smirked while some ladies instigated.

"Bitch, I'll fuck you up! How this ho even know my business?" Gabby said, coming toward me as I stood there. If she wanted a fight, then so fucking be it. I wasn't backing down—win, lose, or draw.

"I know your business because your 'homegirl' told me," I said, pointing at Marissa. "But bitch, if you want a fight, then we can run it. You not finna punk me, pussy ass ho."

"Umm... is there a problem? It can't be, not with this one here," Cassidy said, jumping in front of me.

"Tell yo' friend to watch her mouth before I have to beat her ass," Gabby said while Marissa held her back.

Shit was stupid. I just told her ass how her friend put her business out there and she was steady around her.

"Ho, the day you put hands on me is the same day you'll be picking up all your teeth from the floor. Fuck with me." These bitches hated me for no reason at all. I'd be damned if I was going to let them bully me or think they could. We had to be tough around here with the bitches and niggas. Respect was respect.

"Enough of that. Y'all move the fuck around. It's

money to be made," Cassidy said while some of the girls left out the dressing room. They respected her.

"You got lucky this time, you weak ass bottom-feeder. I'll catch in two weeks once your bodyguard is long gone. Come on, Marissa," Gabby said, leading the way out while her fake ass friend followed.

"You good?" Cassidy said, looking over to me.

Ignoring what she asked me, my mind went back to what Gabby just said. "What did she mean about two weeks and how you'd be gone, Cassidy?"

"Girl, you and I both know how these bitches are. Don't worry about Gabby or that messy ass Marissa," she said, trying to downplay shit.

"Cassidy, don't you bullshit me. Not me outta everybody," I said, pushing her to the side.

She shot me a confused look and then sighed. As I was taking my hands off of her, she spoke. "I'm leaving."

"What?" I couldn't believe my ears.

Cassidy really just said she was leaving the club, and she couldn't even have the decency to inform me. I was the closest person to her at the club, and not only did she look after me since day one, but I actually considered her as a friend. I was hurt.

"See, bitch? This is why I didn't want to tell you. Look

at you. Eyes already watering. Face all red. Yo' light-skin ass look like you 'bouta pass out. I was gonna tell you, really." She shook her head.

"Yeah and when was that again? Bitch, you was ready to disappear, you and your G-string. Fuck you, Cassidy, for real," I said, storming out the door.

Stopping in my tracks, I exhaled sharply. Everybody knew to leave their emotions and feelings at the door. On the floor, we needed to be happy yet still focused. No nigga was tipping an angry and stuck-up ass female. You had to play your cards right if you wanted that bag, and I was all about that.

"Ivy, get yo' ass out there. We got Ross in the building tonight, and that nigga is always generous," Montell said, coming out of nowhere.

"I'll be right there, Montell," I said, annoyed, taking the elevator upstairs.

When I stepped off of the elevator, I saw things were more packed than ever. It made sense. We had a Miami legend in the building.

"You know what Ross drinking on." Nancy the bottle girl approached me while I slightly laughed.

"Of course, Bel Air."

"Make your money, girl."

"I always do," I replied, walking straight to Ross's

section but not before grabbing a few bottles. "What's going on, gorgeous? I was looking for you."

"Hey, Ross. I got those bottles for you," I said, placing them right on ice.

"Your future is bright, baby. Don't ever forget that," he told me, and I smiled.

"You know where to find me if you need anything else."

"Always." He nodded, and I walked away but not before receiving the five stacks he placed in my hand.

Sticking it in my fanny pack, I walked over to the bar. Across the room, I could see Montell having a conversation with Gabby. By the look on her face, I could tell it wasn't good news. Once she looked back at me, she had the meanest glare on her face. I simply blew her a kiss and waved. Whatever happened to her that bitch deserved it.

"You wanna talk now?" Cassidy said, popping up, and I rolled my eyes.

"No the fuck I don't," I said, attempting to walk away from her until she pulled me back.

"You think this shit is easy for me, Ivy? Club Wishes is my home."

"So why are you leaving then?"

"Because ain't shit permanent. Not a damn thing in this

world last forever. What did I tell you when you first came here? What do I tell all these bitches? This place is temporary, and you better have a backup plan, always. My time here is up. I just hope you have the courage to leave when that time comes," she said, walking away and leaving me to think.

I didn't want to spend my whole life here, and I didn't know what God had in store for me, but I damn sure would've told Cassidy that I was leaving.

"I needa drink. Give me a shot of Hennessy please," I told the bartender, Bri.

"You got it."

I watched her fix my shot, and as soon as she pushed it my way, I downed it with no hesitation. Montell wasn't a fan of us drinking on the job unless a customer offered to buy us a drink, but oh fucking well.

"You fuckin' bitch! You did this!" I heard somebody yell, coming closer to me. By the time I turned around, I felt a punch to the face. Quickly catching my balance, I seen Gabby charging at me.

"What the fuck is your problem?" I said, moving to the side.

"You got me fired, ho. I should kill you," she said, now crying and angry.

"Gabby, if you—" I wasn't even able to finish my

sentence, because the dumb ho ran up on me. Now I had no choice but to whoop her ass. Things got out of hand to fast because now we were in the middle of the club throwing blows. The more I whooped her ass, the more I thought about all the bad things that were going on in my life. She tried to make me her punching bag with her words, so I made her my punching bag with my fist.

"You trash ass ho! Don't you ever come at me like that!" I yelled, throwing her to the ground as I banged her head repeatedly into the glass floor.

"Ivy... Oh my God! You're gonna kill her!" Bri yelled, trying to get me off of her.

"Don't touch me! I'm gon' show this ho who the real bully is!" I spat. All I saw was red. I was tired of letting this girl make it. She and the other bitches around here thought they could get over on me. I bet tonight they'd leave me the fuck alone.

"Darren, get yo' ass over here!" I heard Montell shout from afar.

"Get off of me." I kicked as I was pulled off the floor. This was a strong individual unlike Bri because I was unable to escape this grip.

"Ivy, what the fuck were you thinking?" Montell said, getting in my face.

"Me? You can't be fuckin' serious. That bitch is the one who attacked me. Not the other way around."

"I wouldn't give a flying fuck who started what. You bitches tryna give me a lawsuit? Darren, clean this mess up and go get this girl some medical attention. I'll deal with you later, Ms. Ivy," Montell said, giving me a distasteful ass look.

It was just like his old, tired ass to side with somebody over me. Just like these bitches in this club, I was getting tired of him as well.

"Oh, I get it. Maybe if I was sucking your dick like the rest of these bitches in here you would side with me. You know what? Fuck you, Montell! You can go to hell, bastard! I quit, mothafucka!"

"You quit?" Montell laughed, approaching me. "Now you know yo' unstable ass need this job more than ever. I'm doing you a favor. You not done with this club until *I* say so. Get yo' ass out of my sight." He pointed his finger in my face.

I was just about to choke his nasty ass out until I felt myself being lifted off the ground again. *What the fuck?*

The only thing I wanted to do was slap the fuck out of Montell for all the times he disrespected me, and Darren was getting in the way of that—at least I thought he was until I saw Darren on the ground with Gabby.

*Then who…*

"Calm down, shorty. What you getting out of character for?" I heard a familiar male voice say. His voice was so angelic to me. The way his voice boomed in my ears made me melt like butter in his arms. My whole guard was down for about a good twenty seconds. I just felt at peace, believe it or not.

"Ty?" I said, turning around to face him.

Moving his arms down to my waist, he licked his lips and then smiled. "Miss me?" He joked, and I rolled my eyes playfully and then pushed him back or at least tried to. His grip was tight on me, just like I liked it to be when I was in the comfort of my nigga.

What was it with this man? It was like I could never escape him, even if I tried. God knows I tried.

Asking the obvious, I spoke up. "Why are you always popping up, sir?"

"Why are you always into shit, ma'am?" he replied.

"You can't answer a question with a question."

"Just did," he said with dipped eyebrows and a side smirk. Ty was too damn cocky. It made no sense, but I was used to it since every nigga I fucked with had that same demeanor. It was the same thing with these niggas these days. They all wanted to do the same thing—ruin a bitch's life.

Still, I could see how easy it was for a girl to fall for

his chocolate ass. Everything about him screamed fine. He was far from a broke nigga, and something told me he didn't have a problem getting any girl he wanted to. That cocky demeanor went a long way.

"Whatever. Move," I said, pushing him out of my way.

"Ivy, get yo' ass back to work," Montell had the nerve to tell me.

I had to literally laugh in his face. "What part of I quit don't you understand, nigga? The *I* or the fucking *quit*? It's fuck you for life. You don't own me."

This time, the crowd around us got bigger. It was a lit night, which meant more ballers were around, and the last thing Montell wanted was to look weak. He wanted to make it seem like he controlled everything around here.

"Bitch, how many times —"

Ty gently pushed me to the side and walked up on Montell. I couldn't hear their conversation, but I could read faces. Whatever Ty told him made him calm the fuck down real quick and move around.

"Everybody back to work!" he shouted, and everyone did so. Before he walked away, he shot me a look but remained silent.

I wasn't a dummy. This was far from over.

"Come with me," Ty said, telling me more so than

asking me. He already had his hand on my small waist, leading me to the elevator. I could've said fuck no, but I didn't. I did exactly what he told me. I was just going with the flow, I guess.

The whole time in the elevator, I stood there pissed with my arms crossed. I didn't plan my night to go this way, but crazier things happened at this club. It didn't hit me until now that I'd actually quit my job. Sure, I had some racks saved up, but there was so much more money in this club for me. I had to think of something quick and new. I'd be damned if I came back begging for my job. Fuck that, and most importantly, fuck Montell.

"What?" I said, looking over to Ty, who couldn't stop laughing.

"Nothing, you just fine when you mad. Cheer up. It's not the end of the world." He patted my shoulder, and I smacked my lips.

"If you think I'm tripping off this stupid ass job, then you might wanna think again."

"Then what is it then?"

"Tuh. Ty, you in my business? Don't do that," I said, watching the elevator stop and then getting off. The way I stomped around, I knew the devil was mad down below. I didn't even know where I was going. I just knew I needed to get the fuck from Club Wishes quick, fast, and in a hurry.

"Where you going, Ivy?" Ty said, grabbing my hand.

I stopped breathing for a good three seconds. There it was again. His touch, just like his voice, it had an effect on me. His hands were so smooth, which was a shock because I knew he was the type of nigga who got his hands dirty from time to time.

Still, he managed to keep himself up to par. Looking down at his hand on mine, I saw his nails were so clean and perfectly cut down. He was a man that cared for his appearance. Shit, I was convinced this nigga even did facials. There wasn't a bruise or pimple in sight. Ty was beautiful with the perfect features.

"With you," I said, ready to risk it all.

"Huh?" he said, looking down on me while he bit his lip and licked a few of his front teeth. "Home. I'm going home, Ty," I said, finally removing his hand from mine.

"Bet, let me walk you out then," he said as I sighed and ran my hands through my freshly installed twenty-six inches of Malaysian loose wave hair.

"Why?"

"Man, come on," he said, leading the way like he'd done earlier. Just like before, he grabbed my hand, and this time, I made sure to let go of his sooner than later.

"Why you always gotta question shit? I ain't did you no harm yet," he said, looking back at me. "Maybe because I don't know you," I stated the obvious.

"Yeah, well you can get to know me. I ain't all bad."

"All bad, half bad, let's be honest, isn't it all the same?" I thought aloud as soon as we made it outside.

"Don't tell me you ain't got a little bad in you. I seen you out there tonight, wildin'," he said as we stopped walking.

"That wasn't on me. Believe it or not."

Staring deeply in my eyes, he stepped back some and then stuffed his hands into his pocket. "I believe you."

For some reason, I questioned it. Remembering that crazy ass night, he did tell me he had this superpower that allowed him to know when somebody was lying. Maybe that was a good thing because if it was anything different, I would've probably ended up dead.

Nodding my head slowly, I kept quiet until he said something else.

"How come you ain't hit me back that one day?"

"What one day?" I asked, playing dumb.

He smacked his lips. "You know what day, Ivy. Quit insulting my intelligence. That's a red flag, especially if we gon' ever make this work," he said, and my eyes grew wide.

"Make what work?"

"You seen my text. Why not respond?"

One thing I noticed about Ty was if he didn't want to answer a question, then he simply wouldn't. He was good for changing the subject or answering a question with a question. I decided to let that last statement ride and move on.

"There was nothing to say."

When I got that text from Ty, I was confused. Even standing in front of him, I still was. I had so many questions: how did he get my number? Or why did he feel comfortable enough to reach out to me? What did Ty want from me?

"How you figure that? The way I see it, we had a lot to talk about. We still have a lot to discuss." "I don't know what you mean." I shrugged and moved my head from side to side.

"I seen the way you looked at me at Kordell's welcome home party. You was shocked to see me—you were afraid," he said in a low tone. Lifting my chin from the ground, he spoke to me. "You don't gotta be afraid of me, Ivy."

It seemed like he actually cared what I thought and how I felt about him. I could tell that brought an uneasy feeling to him because, for the first time tonight, he couldn't even look me in my eyes for a long period of time. I was just here to tell him my opinion of him didn't matter and it never would.

"Of course I was taken back. I thought I would never have to see you again. I planned not to, but it's like I can't escape you. It's too damn weird."

He couldn't expect me to be jumping for joy when it came to him. He might have spared my life, but he still wasn't the number-one person on my list these days. Things could've went left, and every time I look at him, it's a constant reminder on how I could've been taken from Kacey. It wasn't a good feeling.

"Weird…"

"Weird because you kidnapped me and could've killed me."

"Okay, but I didn't," Ty spoke in an insensitive ass tone that I didn't like too much.

At times, he could come off as sweet, and then the next minute, he was being that demanding ass nigga. I caught on quick to him, and I hated it.

He grabbed my arms gently and backed me against the wall. There was barely any space in between us, so right now, his face was fairly close to mine. The closer he was to me, the more I admired his presence, mainly his lips. I swore it felt like my heart was beating outside of my chest.

"You scared of me, Ivy?" he gently spoke, squinting his eyes some. His stares were so strong that they put me in a trance.

Unable to speak or move, I played it cool and allowed

him to do whatever he wanted to do to me. He wouldn't hurt me, stranger or not. My intuition told me that.

Feeling the heat rise between my thighs, I knew I had to get away from this man quickly. Those intensive stares from a fine man always led me to do things that I regretted. I learned from the past that it was all about doing things differently this time around.

Barely able to get my words out, I parted my lips slowly and then spoke. "Bye, Ty." I moved around him and started to walk in the direction of valet parking.

"I'm starting to think you like for a nigga to chase you down. I'ma only do that one time, heads-up for the next time. Come here," he said, pulling me close to him. The scent of his cologne made my insides tingle. I could've fallen into his arms at any given moment. A part of me wanted him to make the first move, so I would have an excuse to know what it felt like being in his arms. *If only.*

"I don't want no bad blood between us. You Kordell's people, and that's my nigga fo' sho, so you good with me. I can't tell you to let that shit go that went down between us. If you wanna hold on to it, then do that, just know we good on my end. Alright?" he said.

I nodded my head slowly. I didn't know what was happening in my head, but whenever this man spoke to me, I was intrigued.

"Drive home safely, Ivy," Ty said about to walk off until I grabbed his arm.

"Wait... Why didn't you do it?"

"Do what? Kill you?" he asked, and I nodded once more. He quickly responded, "There was no need to."

The way he had no hesitation at all to answer my question assured me that he was being truthful. He didn't have to think about it because he meant what he said.

"I believe you," I said, making him laugh some.

As soon as I made it back to Club Wishes, all I could think about was why Ty didn't kill me. He was well capable of doing so. It wasn't hard to catch on to his job description one bit. If he was a real street nigga, then nine times out of ten, he would have to kill. Ty was a boss though, so whenever he actually got his hands dirty, the shit was personal. I might have not known him personally, but it wasn't hard for a girl like me to read between the lines.

"That's good to know. So I got a feeling I'ma see you around again."

"Someway, somehow, you always seem to, right?" I smirked, turning in my tracks. I didn't hear footsteps going into the other direction, so I turned back around. Ty was still standing there, watching me precisely. The look he gave me screamed he wanted to fuck me—scratch that, he wanted to take me down right there, right then in the parking lot.

Little did he know, it would never go there between us. I had bigger fish to fry, like the fact I had no damn job. Fucking around with him was only going to set me back, or so I thought.

# *Breeze*

"Ball, nigga. I'm wide open," I said, raising my arms in the air while my cousin, Dom, passed me the ball. We'd been at the court for hours, just hooping on niggas. This was my everyday schedule if I wasn't out trapping or caught up in some shit.

"That's game, nigga. Run me my three stacks please. I need all my shit in twenties if you got it," Dom shouted right as I made that three-pointer. We were playing a three-on-three game with some other niggas from around the way, and of course, we won. Every time I was on the court, I made a mothafucka wish they didn't go against me, and if they did, they'd have to take that L, respectfully.

"Damn, man, ain't no way y'all should've won that game," George said, digging into his pockets and pulling out some cash.

"Nah, I'm good, G. You know I don't do it for the money." I politely turned him down. It was true, most of the homies played for bread, but basketball was never about the money to me. I had plenty of that. I played the game because I loved it. I loved it so much I planned to go to college on a full scholarship, but shit happens, right?

"Well, shit, I do. Run me my money expeditiously,"

Dom said, patting his hand while I laughed some.

"This nigga."

"How 'bout we play again, double or nothing. Y'all know I'm good for it," George said.

"Aye, you really wanna take that L again, nigga? I mean, it is yo' money, and I can't get enough of that. You down, Breeze?" Dom asked, tapping my shoulder. He always made sure I was on his team at all times.

He and I together were like D. Wade and LeBron James. Nobody was fucking with us, and when we were teens, we stayed whooping ass from kids to the OGs. The money was good, but it was nothing like that drug money. That shit would really buy you what you want.

"I ain't got shit else to do I'm with—second thought, that rematch gon' have to wait." Changing my mind, my eyes averted to across the court. A big smile appeared on my face when I saw Ni aka my favorite sight to see.

"Huh? What you mean? You know I got them child support payments coming up, and you gon' do this," Dom complained.

"My bad, bro, but you on your own," I said, jogging over to my water bottle and towel and then across the way to Ni.

"Oh, I see how it is, nigga. Remember that," Dom

yelled from a distance while I ignored him. The only thing I was worried about was speaking to Aniya. We hadn't really talked in a few months, and I missed her more than anything. It wasn't the same between us ever since we broke up, but I'd always have love for her. I'd always be in love with her I'm convinced, and I was okay with that the idea.

The closer I got to her, I realized what she was doing. She sat under a tree on a blanket reading a book. She wore a tan dress that hugged her body just right with a pair of all white Chanel slides. The white hat she wore on her head was so big it blocked the sun from her eyes as well as the big ass tree she was sitting under. She looked peaceful. Too bad a nigga was about to disturb that. We were good for that.

"What you over here reading, my songbird?" I spoke successfully, getting her attention.

She looked up at me and then rolled her eyes. There it was, that attitude that I loved and hated at the same damn time. It didn't even matter though, because I was just happy to be in her presence. She was so fine, and I hadn't seen her face to face in a minute.

"Don't call me that. You know I don't sing anymore."

"Well, you should. You have a beautiful voice. May I?" I said, motioning to the seat next to her while she laughed some.

"If I say no you're still gonna sit anyways, so…"

"You're right," I said, taking the seat next to her. I couldn't help but stare at her. Ni was not only beautiful on the outside but in the inside as well. She wasn't like them other girls out there. She was in tune with herself mentally, physically, and spiritually, and it'd been that way since the beginning. I loved everything about her from her beautiful brown skin to her style and voice. She was perfect to me. She was born with a perfect heart. My only regret is that I couldn't protect it.

"Christian, what do you want? I'm trying to study," she said, making me break out of my thoughts. It was so easy to get caught up in them when she was the topic of discussion. In the streets, you could never get over on me, but damn I had a soft spot for Ni.

"I can't see what you up to now? You already act like you can't hit a nigga up sometimes." Yeah, I wanted to be back with Ni, but I also knew that shit wouldn't just happen overnight. I wasn't just going to give up my lifestyle, and she wasn't going to forgive me that quick for everything that took place between us. Still, did that mean we couldn't communicate like we used to? I just couldn't see how people walked away from a person they loved like that. The way I saw it, we were meant to be in each other's life. She was my friend before anything. I wasn't ashamed to say I needed her in all aspects.

"I know you're good. Social media tells me everything I need to know." She shrugged, and I smacked my lips.

"Social media don't know shit. They don't know the truth behind the good life." Instagram, Facebook, Twitter, whatever, it was all just apps that people got on for entertainment. Ninety percent of those people weren't happy with themselves or their life. They used those apps as an escape, a place to lie and hide from their insecurities. The only reason people enjoyed that shit was because it gave them an image.

I didn't give a fuck about that, because at the end of the day, I was *really* living like that on and offline. I wasn't even a social media ass nigga, yet mothafuckas knew how I was coming. That was my whole point. They only saw what I allowed them to, and there was no way they'd catch me online in my feelings, crying over shit. I couldn't even see how people went on live just to cry. That shit was pussy. I'd slap the shit out my family just for playing games like that on the internet.

"So what's the truth then?" she said, closing her book and looking over to me, giving me all her attention. I liked it this way.

"Truth is I miss you."

Ni smiled and shook her head. "Boy, if I had a dollar for every time you told me that, then I'd be the richest woman on earth." She joked and nudged my shoulder. "Eww, you're so sweaty, Christian," she squealed while she wiped her hands on the blanket she sat on.

"I just got done ballin' at the court. What you expect? You know how official yo' man is out there," I said as she frowned.

"My man?" she asked with a confused expression on her face.

"That's what I said, right?"

Instead of speaking up, she remained silent, slightly laughed, then opened up her book, and started reading again.

"What you reading, Ni?" I said, scooting closer to her. I thought about wrapping my arm around her shoulder, but I didn't need her to ho me like I was musty and hurt my pride. Fuck that.

"A little something, something."

"Let me see." Taking the black-and-white covered book from her, I scanned the cover and immediately smiled. "Love languages, huh?"

"Yeah, what you know about it?" Ni smiled back.

"Shit, a lot. In fact, more than you think." I smirked, and she started to blush.

"Whatever."

"I'm serious, Ni. I know what it's like to be in love. I was in love with you, still am," I admitted to her, even though she already knew that. Reassurance was never our problem because at the end, of the day she knew she had my heart.

Our problems had more to do with disagreements. We had a lot of them, jumping into a full commitment at just seventeen. Fast forward to now, we were still young in disagreements, so not much had changed.

"Why you looking at me like that?" She glared at me.

"Because I'm waiting to hear you say it back." I knew what it was, but I'd never get tired of hearing the girl I loved tell me she loved me just as much. That shit brought joy to me for many reasons, one being I couldn't get love from anybody in this world like I could with Aniya, and another being this world was so fucked up. Holding on to that four-letter word was what kept people going sometimes, if we believed it or not.

"If I told you I loved you, what would that do? What would it change? Nothing." She tried shutting me down.

I sucked my teeth and shook my head. "'Cause you not ready for that conversation just yet. It's cool though. I'ma let you do you. You'll be right back when the timing is right," I confidently stated.

Whoever I fucked with, I left a mark on. That was how deep my presence was. I had bitches falling in love with me, and that was never the road I wanted to drive on. It was simply relations for me, nothing more nothing less. I wasn't looking for anything serious with these females, and they knew that. If they chose to stick around and get fucked on cool, but if they decided they wanted more and wanted to cut me off, then, hey, that was cool too. It was way too much pussy in the world for me to even get attached.

Hence, my connection with Aniya. It wasn't about the sex with her. Granted, it was damn good every time, but I longed for something way more with her. Stability. I actually wanted to take the time and be around her. She didn't annoy me like the others. I was interested in all of her—mind, body, and soul—and when the time was right, she'd be the one I settled down with.

"I'm starting to think you forgot the reason I even broke up with yo' ass. See, the difference between me and those other girls is I know the real," she said, coming closer to me. She grabbed my chin and looked me directly in my eyes. A little above a whisper, she spoke. "I know the timing won't ever be right with you."

Looking right back at her, it wasn't that I wanted to know why she said what she said it was that I needed to know.

Could she really feel that way about me, a nigga who genuinely loved and wanted to be with her? This was me we were talking about. "What makes you so sure?"

Aniya sighed and then closed her eyes for a few seconds. I could tell she was deciding if she wanted to say what came to her mind. I wasn't a person she had to lie to. She could always keep it real with me. I could take it.

"Christian, I've moved on, and most importantly, I'm with someone else."

"I don't give a fuck, Aniya. Fuck that pussy ass nigga."

Her mouth dropped for a few seconds like she was shocked about what I said. Standing up, she looked down at me and laughed slightly. "You don't even—you know what? You haven't changed one bit. Still that same selfish, inconsiderate ass little boy you've always have been... making those same ass stupid mistakes. You could've been more. You could've had a better life. You could've had me! Does that not mean anything to you?"

"It means a lot to me, but I don't think you'll ever understand that," I admitted. "Or at least you not tryna hear it. Which one is it?"

"Tuh, I'm not about to answer that. If you really cared about me, why? Why did you choose to take another route? Things were good. You were making good grades. You were about to go ball in LA on a full scholarship. You were a top pick. We would talk every day. You had me," she said, squatting on the side of me. "You know how many men— black men at that—wished they were in your position?"

"Just leave it alone, alright?" I could see it in Aniya's eyes that she was concerned about me. She wanted answers, but I couldn't give her any right now. I owed her explanation for my sudden transformation. I was just scared of what she would think of me. Scared that she would judge me for all the fucked-up things I did in this world. Lord knows I couldn't take them back. A part of me didn't want to, really.

She was right. Things were good back then. I had a plan to be something more than what I was, but things changed. She should know all about change, considering the fact that she called herself fucking with another nigga.

A look of devastation washed over her face, and then she took her same spot. She didn't look at me. Instead, her gaze was focused ahead. I knew she was thinking, but about what?

"We'll never be the same Christian, ever," she spoke up after a while.

"That's how you really feel, Aniya?"

"Being with you is taking a step back, and I won't do that. You had plenty of chances to tell me the truth, and you didn't. If you loved and cared for me like you say you do, then you would've came to me with the truth. I would never do that to you. I've always been an open book. Have I not?"

"Yeah, you have."

"So what do you expect? You want me to just forgive you with no questions asked, leave my guy, and accept you and all your flaws?"

"Can't tell you what to do, but damn, talk about wishful thinking, baby." I slightly chuckled, kissing her forehead. "See you around, Ni. You know where to find me. You know how to contact me," I said, standing while she remained silent and opened her book back up. I wanted to stay and chop it up with her, but all that was going to do was lead to an argument. I wasn't giving up on her. I would never. She was my soul mate. Aniya just needed time, and I was going to give her that.

"And apparently they do too. Answer that call away from me. I don't want that type of energy anywhere close to me," she said, referring to my ringing phone, it was Ty.

There was no doubt he was calling about work, which meant I had to really go. I think we were all serious about our bread. That shit just couldn't wait.

"I can handle whatever truth you throw my way." Aniya grabbed my phone from my hand. She was starting to get irritated by me, and on the inside, I was smiling because I knew she still cared. That was the only reason why she was going so hard for answers. Still, some things were better left unsaid. I understood that.

"No, you can't." I assured her as I grabbed her shoulder gently. "Can I have my phone back?"

Aniya sighed and stepped back some. "Here," she said, handing me my phone. She stood with her arms crossed, waiting for me to say something else, but I had nothing for her right now. One day, we would have all the time in the world to discuss everything… one day. "Christian, you've changed…"

"I know. Don't be a stranger, Ni," I replied to her for the last time.

Respecting her wishes, I waited until I was a few feet away from her to answer my phone. "What's good, Ty?"

"Aye, meet me at the trap in ten, Breeze. We got a problem."

It could've been anything. That was just how it was. When that phone rang, I was off handling what had to be done. Truth was, every time I got a phone call from my niggas, I expected the worse.

Aniya knew what she was talking about when she said I changed. I did. Before, I could only see myself dribbling a ball and making shots and shit. Now, I was busting guns and moving work like it was nothing. I knew she wanted me to go back, but I couldn't. I was in way too deep. She probably thought she could save me, but you see, I knew the truth... I knew I was going to die in these streets if anything.

"On the way." I hung up.

## Ty

"You sure you don't want me to handle this shit? Say the word, and I'm on go, Ty," Rodney blurted out after a moment of us sitting in silence.

We were at the trap in my office, and my mind had been racing. The only thing I could do was sit in silence and try to think of what my next move would be. I was at Vanessa's crib getting the wildest head I could imagine from her, and boom, my phone rang, and it was Rodney on my line, talking about some surprising ass news regarding business. If it wasn't one thing, it was a fucking other. I just had to handle Mikey's disloyal ass, and now, here we are once again. Pure bullshit I tell you.

Inhaling the smoke from my blunt, I shook my head. "We'll handle this shit together, Rodney, as a team," I spoke, releasing the smoke from my nose and mouth.

This wasn't a shoot first, ask questions later type of situation. We needed to get all information intact. I was talking no loose ends or none of that shit. This was business, *our* business. It doesn't get more serious than that.

"All I'm saying is too much flaw shit is going on right underneath our nose. The fuck is happening? It's not likely to get one up on this side." Rodney began to pace.

"Nigga, sit down. All that pacing got my nerves bad."

On the outside, it might've appeared that I was calm, but it was definitely the weed. On the inside, I wanted to pull a Rodney and leave a nigga's head on the pavement, but that wouldn't be happening for one reason—logic. At all times, I'd play it smart. I was an advocate for being low key and getting shit done like it needed to be. Sometimes things went a little unplanned though, nevertheless, I was always one step ahead. There was a solution for this problem, and I was going to handle it.

"We'll talk about it more when Breeze get here." I didn't like going over anything when somebody on the team was missing. I felt it was disrespectful and hated repeating myself.

Rodney, Breeze, and I were a trio. We made moves together, we looked out for each other, and we weren't selfish. That was why we were on top. That was why we would stay on top. There was no amount of money or status going to change that.

Rodney smacked his lips. "Man, where that little nigga at anyways? I know you told him it was urgent. I'm ready to get shit done now."

"Rodney, shut the fuck up please. If he say he on his way, then he on his way." Hotheaded wasn't the only thing

Rodney was. The nigga was also impatient.

Breeze was the youngest out of the crew, and Rodney was the oldest. I could see why the two of them went back and forth a lot of the times, but shit, what brothers didn't? That was natural. I'd admit, sometimes, I worried about Breeze. He was only twenty-one years old and so deep into these streets. Not only that, but he was a good kid with a great future ahead of him. Believe it or not. I turned him down several times when he asked me if he could come work with me. I guess the eighth time just hit different because here he was now on the side of me, helping bring in plenty of money. The little nigga was smart as hell. He knew the game.

I knew he was destined for this shit when I purposely gave him some bullshit ass pounds of weed that wasn't hitting on shit to sell. Imagine my surprise when he came back with no weed left over and twice as much of profit than expected. Yeah, Breeze had his heart set on this game. He was in it for the long run, and I could damn sure count on him every time.

"Alright, Ty, but we could be out there doing something right fuckin' now, and you know it," he said.

I started to roll another blunt up. The one I was smoking wasn't even halfway gone yet, but shit, I knew I was going to need it.

"I came as soon as I could. What's going on?" Breeze

said, bursting into my office covered with sweat.

"Damn, nigga. Where you come from? Running a damn mile or something?" I wondered.

"Nah, he was probably hooping. He want the best of both worlds. Just call him a hood superstar." Rodney sarcastically laughed.

Breeze shook his head and speed walked to the seat across from me. "I don't got time for the jokes. If y'all wanted me to flame y'all ass up, I could've did that over the phone. So again, the fuck is going on?"

Getting straight to it, I stopped rolling my weed and looked at Rodney and then Breeze. "We gotta find somewhere else to clean our drug money. Both the hair salon and blowing alley is a wrap."

Breeze looked at me confused and then at Rodney. Taking a few minutes to process what I'd just said, he spoke up. "Huh? Ain't no way. I just went to the alley three days ago and everything was cool. The fuck went wrong, and the hair salon too? Nah." He shook his head.

"Somebody called in a few complaints about the alley, so we're under investigation. I'm not saying fuck it, but for now, we gotta move around."

To be this drug game, one would have had a few spots to cover your tracks. We had a few places individually and together, but the alley was where we made most of our bread. That and the hair salon. Bitches paid the most to get their hair done, which meant the set up and hair equipment was expensive. It was perfect until it wasn't anymore.

"And what about the salon? I thought yo' bitch was in charge of that," Breeze said, looking over to Rodney.

"She is, mothafucka. Clearly, it's some funny shit going on. Whole three years her shit been open, ain't nothing ever pop off, but last night, her shit get vandalized upside down. I'm telling y'all, somebody tryna stop this shit we got going, and we needa get to the bottom of it before it get worse," Rodney said still standing.

"So you question her about this shit, or you let her slide 'cause you supplying dick to her?" Breeze questioned Rodney as he twisted his lip.

"Breeze, you sound dumb as hell. Of course I questioned her ass. It ain't like that's my bitch anyways. Just my baby mama. I know when she lying, and that's not the case this time. She know better. I'd fuck her up about my bread," Rodney stated.

One of Rodney's baby mamas, April, owned a hair salon with the help of Rodney of course. The arrangement was simple. He let her do hair and make her money while we cleaned our money through the shop. Things were running smoothly, like I liked them to be. Business lasted for a while, and everything was the way I needed it to be. I mean, I wasn't worried about a damn thing. Rodney's baby mama wasn't going to pass up no opportunity like this. She was laced in all the finer things she could imagine because of us, so I knew her ass wouldn't dare try to cross us and ruin that. Only a fool would. Yeah, something else was definitely up. I just didn't know yet.

"What the fuck. What we gon' do?" Breeze said, wiping the sweat from his head and on his basketball shorts.

"Shoot first, ask questions later, that's my motto," Rodney said, taking the blunt from my hand.

I almost put him on his ass for that shit, but I let him slide. He didn't work good under pressure. I saw it a million times.

Ignoring him just like me, Breeze spoke up. "I mean, we could always clean the money elsewhere. True, the alley and salon were the most beneficial places for us, but we got options."

"We do, but honestly, I'm thinking bigger."

As soon as Rodney gave me the call about what was going down my brain immediately started to think, *what's next?* I had a plan, a plan that would make up for our setbacks. A plan that would bring in way more money than we were making before.

"What's bigger than the salon and the alley, nigga? You got a master plan like that? I needa hear that shit today. Don't get me wrong, you my mans fifty grand, but make me a believer in this bitch," Rodney said, taking two drags of my blunt and then passing it back.

"I'm all ears, Ty." Breeze shrugged his shoulders and waited for my response.

"Y'all niggas trust me, right?"

"You know this," Rodney replied.

Breeze did the same. "With my life."

"Then that's all I needa hear. Give me a couple of days. That's all I need, and I'll have shit worked out. Until then, Rodney you keep your ears to the streets, and Breeze, you continue to make sure everybody doing their job at the trap." What I had planned had to work. I didn't see it going any other way but in my favor.

"I can do that. You think Mikey had something to do with this shit? He was moving sneaky." Breeze shook his head while I sighed and did the same.

Mikey was the first person I thought about in regard to this mess. It just made sense. If you would steal from me, then there was no putting anything past you, simple. But it wasn't like we could ask the dead a question. Right now, we were

IVY & TY: LOVE WASN'T MEANT FOR A DOPE BOY

clueless and would have to wait and see who was behind all of this.

"I wouldn't put shit past a mothafucka, especially his snake ass, but ain't like we can ask him now. I had to dead that fuck nigga, so I did. Only way we gon' ask him anything is if we join him on the other side, and I'll be damned." Rodney said.

"We'll figure it out. We always do," I said, and Breeze looked like he wanted to say something but didn't.

"Coo'. Hit me for anything. I'm finna get up outta here. I gotta stop by the block, and I got this female at my crib by herself. She probably checking a nigga boxers by now," Rodney said, dapping me and then Breeze up.

"Handle yo' shit, king crab," Breeze said while I burst out laughing.

"What I tell you, Breeze? Stop putting extra STDs on me for real."

"Nigga, you had one, you had them all. Fuck outta my face." Breeze stood as I did the same.

"Nah, y'all don't start. Both of y'all mothafuckas can slide. I ain't tryna hear y'all go back and forth, not today," I said, ending the back-and-forth before it could even start.

"You right. I'm not finna argue with a nigga who got less than ten bodies on him. I'm out," Rodney said, heading out the door.

"And that's why you burning now, bitch!" Breeze shouted as I shook my head. Every time we linked, the two of them were laughs.

"Breeze, take yo' ass home just like him," I said, grabbing my phone and car keys off my desk. I wasn't going home just yet. I planned to meet with my lawyer about a few things pertaining business. It was always a smart move to have the right legal support behind you at all times, especially because in this game, you never knew when things would backfire. Jim, my lawyer, was the best of the best in Miami. He wasn't useful to a broke nigga though. I could tell you that much.

"I am, after I go see that these workers putting in work out there. After that, I'm going straight to the crib, right?" he asked me with a reassuring expression.

I knew what that was all about. He wanted to do more, but there was only so much we could do right now with little information.

"Right, Breeze. Take yo' ass home," I told him, and he sighed.

"Yeah, alright, Ty."

"Wasn't you balling anyways? Go back to doing that," I said as we both walked out of my office before I locked it.

"I was. Ran into Ni too. She got a new nigga now," he said, looking over to me.

"So? Fuck that nigga." I shrugged, and he agreed with me.

"I said the same damn thing."

"Yeah, well, I hope you ain't looking to yo' big brother for no relationship advice, because all I'ma tell you is to focus on your hustle and never get attached to no female. They temporary just like pussy, no matter how good it is. They always seem to get attached. That's why you gotta cut them off eventually," I said, and he smacked his lips.

"It's not like that with me and her though." He called himself trying to tell me.

"Don't matter if it is or ain't. Shit will never work, and you know that. Stop stressing over things that you can't change, Breeze. That's my advice."

"Bro, I swear I can't talk to you and damn sure not Rodney about stuff like this," he complained all the way to our whips.

"You want honesty, right? So I'ma give it to you. You young as hell. What you worried about one female for anyways? Enjoy your life, and then when you wanna settle down in about ten years, I might just pull up to the wedding with a nice gift—shackles." I joked, and we laughed.

"See? That's that shit I be talking about, Ty. I'm gone," Breeze said, getting into his car while I continued to laugh.

"I'ma fuck with you later," I told him. Sitting in my Maybach, all I could think was how so far gone little bro was over this one girl. Love must've run deep with him. Fuck that, it did. We didn't call him lover boy Breeze for nothing. His nose was wide open, and I knew for a fact I never wanted to go that route. It was too much. If you asked me, I could never get tired of fucking who I wanted to with no strings attached.

Halfway to my lawyer's office, he hit me, saying we would have to meet up at a later time since he got caught up in a meeting. He knew my conversations were mostly always urgent, so I wasn't too happy that we would have to reschedule, nevertheless, I agreed, and that was that. I started to just head to the crib, but I got hungry, so I went to my soul food joint to go grab something to eat.

Kim's was a hundred percent mine. I named it after my mother. She might've been on that healthy wave now, but everything about her was soulful and so was the food. I had the best cooks in that bitch, the scenery was nice with the perfect view, and we had the best customer service. This place made me a lot of money, but I refused to bring any of my drug money into it. Kim's was a thousand percent clean, and I planned on keeping it that way.

My mother understood that herself, and she was happy that I chose to keep it that way. Still, she knew how her son was—committed to the game. She accepted me though, always and through whatever. For that reason, I'd give her the world. Anything she wanted or needed, I was there. Even when I was dead and gone, she'd be set for life. My mother was my heart. Without her, I was nothing. Her blood was running through me, and it didn't get any better than that.

"Hey, Mr. Dorsey. You want your regular?" Carla, the cashier, greeted me as soon as I walked in the door.

"What's good, Carla? Gone 'head and hook me up. You know what I like," I said, and she smiled.

"Got you."

While she got my order together, I took a seat in one of the booths to the side. It was going on three on a weekday, and that was usually when we got busy each day, so I was prepared to see folks coming in and out of here real soon.

Right when I pulled my phone from my pocket, I saw Vanessa calling me. I left her crib before the trap and told her I'd hit her later on. Maybe she misunderstood me because here she was, on my line, like she couldn't comprehend. Still, I picked up for anyways.

"What's up, V?"

"Hey, baby. What you doing?" she asked me as I sat

back and ran a hand over my waves.

I needed to sit in somebody chair ASAP. I never went that long when it came to making sure I kept myself up. I couldn't stand a dirty ass nigga. I had the bread to make sure I was looking damn good all the time. I wasn't cocky or no shit like that—nah, scratch that—I was. I was also one handsome ass nigga, and I put that on my daddy. It didn't get any better than me, but if you wanted to settle down, then I wasn't the man for you.

"Coolin', finna eat. What's up?"

"I was just thinking about you. And I wanted to let you know I won't be able to do dinner tomorrow with you. Something came up last minute that I can't get out of. Sorry."

"It ain't no problem, V. Do you."

"Okay, I was just letting you know—wait, you're not gonna ask me what's going on or why I really can't make it?" she said, sounding a little hurt.

I didn't get it though. I didn't like for her to question me on anything I was doing, so why would I question her? If she said she couldn't make it to dinner, then that was what it was. Was I supposed to feed deeper into it? She couldn't have thought that. I wasn't the type to do that, ever.

"Nah, you said something came up last minute, right? That's good enough for me. I'm not trippin', shorty. You know me," I calmly spoke.

Vanessa got quiet on the phone for a good minute. "Okay, Ty. I just felt the need to tell you," she spoke in a saddened tone. For a split second, she even sounded like she was crying or at least like she wanted to.

Me and Vanessa went way back. Sometimes she could get extremely clingy, but at the end of the day, she knew her place. She knew what I was going for and what I wasn't. It was just lately, things between us had been getting a little weird because of her. I just couldn't put my finger on the problem. I even tried to avoid asking her what was up with her just because I didn't want to hear her say what I thought she was thinking about—us getting serious. I liked Vanessa, even had some love for her, but I couldn't get down like that. I had way too much going on to be settled down with her.

I wasn't completely a heartless ass nigga though. A part of me did really want to know why Vanessa sounded the way she did on the phone right now, so I asked. "Why you sound so sad, Vanessa?"

"I don't know… I can't explain it. I'd rather talk to you face-to-face to be honest. I need to look into your eyes," she said, leaving me slightly confused.

"We was just together earlier though. Why not tell me what you needed to then?"

"The timing didn't feel right. Ty, when you have the chance, you should come over so we can really talk... you know."

"You acting strange, and I'm not really fucking with it, but if you wanna talk in person, then I'm cool with that. Just let me know when, and I'll see if I'm free," I told her.

"I would really love that, so I'll let you know, okay?"

"Okay. V, take care of yourself." I could feel it in my gut that something wasn't right. It kind of worried me.

Vanessa wasn't the type to ever be in some shit. She had her own everything—crib, cars, designer, and she even had a nice job at the bank. She was always happy. She screamed self-sufficient, so this vibe right here she was giving me wasn't her, and I damn sure wasn't used to it.

"You too." She hung up.

"Mr. Dorsey, your order is ready," Carla said, walking over to me with a bag full of the finest food Miami had to offer.

"Everything in here?" I asked her as I scanned through my bag myself.

"Yes, sir. Fried ribs, fried shrimp, greens, macaroni and cheese, and a dinner roll. I got you." Carla slightly laughed.

"Good looking out. That's why I pay you the big bucks."

"Tuh, I'm already knowing. Oh shit… I forgot your sweet tea. Be right back," she said on her way back to the kitchen. "Here you go, sir. They made it extra sweet for you," Carla said, approaching me with that same smile she always had on her face anytime I was around.

"'Preciate it," I said, meeting her halfway.

Right when I got back to my seat, I took a sip of my drink. It was hitting just the way I needed it to. I didn't give a fuck. If I went to a restaurant and their tea wasn't as sweet as I needed it to be, I'd gladly add as much sugar as possible. Shit, it was called sweet tea for a reason, right?

"Yeah, this that shit," I said to myself, nodding my head.

"Yooooo, what's up. This yo' spot or something, nigga? Everybody been telling me about this bitch," Kordell said, approaching me as I slightly laughed.

"What's good with you, K?" I stood, dapping him up as he did the same.

"Shit, coolin', hungry as hell," he said, looking over to the menu.

"I got you. Carla," I shouted her name, and she came right over.

"Yes, Mr. Dorsey?"

"Hook my family up with a little bit of everything

please. It's on the house," I told her.

"Sure thing. I'll be right back."

"On the house? Yeah, this gotta be yo' shit. What you ain't doing, Ty?" Kordell sat down, and I joined him.

"Never stopping, when it comes to this money."

"Aye! I heard that."

It didn't matter if I stopped selling drugs tomorrow. I'd still have money in the bank, and I'd still be profiting from many other things. The dope game wasn't my only hustle. I had a backup plan. It didn't matter if you thought you needed one or not, better safe than sorry around here. I was never going broke, me or my niggas, and I put that on everything.

"You feel me? What you been up to, K? I ain't really chop it up with you since the welcome home party." It was good to see my nigga back home, but that welcome home party turned into something I didn't expect. I mean, I expected food, family, and fun but not all the drama that took place. It wasn't my business to speak on though. That was why I didn't bring it up when I ran into Ivy at the club.

"Catching up with family. I been chillin' really. Tryna make me some little ones on the cool." He shrugged, and I laughed. "For real, nigga. My girl gotta be pregnant by now. I just know it," Kordell said, sounding sure of it.

"I ain't mad at you. A little K running around... That's

what's up."

"That's what I'm saying," he said as Carla came out with a plate of food. "Damn, this how y'all doing it over here?" Kordell said, looking over to me while I threw my hands up.

The food at my spot not only looked good, but it tasted good as well. We were one of the top restaurants around, and it'd been like that since I opened this place up a few years ago.

"What you want to drink? Carla got you."

"Lemonade is fine," Kordell said as Carla did her thing. "So what made you wanna open up a soul food spot, Ty, outta everything?"

"Man, I honestly don't know. I just did that shit, and it's been a success. Plus, you know the game. You know why it's important to have these legit spots," I said, watching Carla bring Kordell his drink.

"Of course." Kordell nodded his head before he said grace and started to eat his food.

I was going to take mine to go, but fuck it. I might as well eat now while I chopped it up with the homie.

"You still been thinking about what you wanna do?" I said, referring to coming back to the game. I wasn't pressuring him, but I hadn't spoken to him since his welcome home party. I was just curious on if his feelings changed.

"I been trying to avoid thinking about that shit. You

and I both know it's not about the money, but still, a part of me feel like I'll always have a place in this game, on the block or not."

"That's some real shit, K. I feel the same way." I wasn't going to find a job that paid as good as the drug game, and even if I did, it was like would I want to even quit? I'd be honest, I couldn't see it happening. I could be a cliché and say selling drugs was all I knew, but I'd be lying to myself if I did. I could've been doing something else, but why? I hadn't heard a valid reason yet, nor did I enter a situation where I would have to quit.

"Nothing else feels right. I told my shorty that, and she like how I know if I don't try, but it's like I know me. I'm caught between a rock and a hard place for real."

I could relate to K in some ways but not all. I didn't have a girl in my ear telling me to stop trapping, even Vanessa never tried to pull that card with me, so I was really clueless when it came to shit like that. That let alone was a reason I wasn't talking commitment with anybody. It was hard for people to accept the real you, and I'd be damned if I allowed somebody to judge me. They couldn't. Fuck them and their thoughts. That was how I felt about it.

"Well, you know what I'ma say—"

"Yeah, some bullshit," K said, cutting me off. "You

ain't worth shit when it comes to relationship advice, but yo' establishment got some good ass food though. I'll give you that."

"Aye, and I'll take it." I shrugged as he laughed and shook his head.

"I'ma figure it out. Wherever my heart leads me, I guess," he said, and I nodded.

"No doubt." I spoke, finally digging into my food.

# Ivy

"Come on, birthday girl. We're on a schedule. There's only so much you can do in a day when you decide to sleep until three," Jai said, hitting me with a pillow repeatedly.

I mean, just fuck my lash extensions, right? If I slept this late, then it was for a reason. I wasn't looking forward to my birthday this year. I was single and another year older, which wasn't really exciting for me, so I would rather today be very chill for me.

"See, I knew I shouldn't have spent the night over here last night. It was a setup. You not slick, Jai," I said, throwing my head under a pillow.

All yesterday, Jai called my phone telling me to come spend a night because she was bored. I should've known that was cap. Her ass was never bored at home, especially since Kordell was back. She just wanted to make sure I spent my birthday the way she would want to spend hers—a classy day and a ratchet night.

"Oh whatever, bitch, get up. The hair, nail, and wax lady is on the way now. You know they charge by the minute. Chop, chop. I got a chef down there making lunch and everything," she said, surprising me but not really. It didn't matter whose birthday it was, Jai always felt like she had to be the one to get the birthday girl or boy drunk and make sure they were having the time of their life. She was just sweet like that.

"Give me a second. Can I get dressed first?" I said, sitting up and grabbing my phone from the nightstand on the left of me. There were many notifications from a few of my family and even my child's father.

"What you have on is fine. It's not like we going outside just yet. Brush your teeth and wash your face, then meet me downstairs, okay? You got ten minutes, or I will be back," she said, sounding like somebody's mama.

"What you mean outside yet? Jainice what do you have planned?" I curiously asked her as she smiled innocently.

"That's for me to know and you to find out, miss mamas, so again, get yo' ass up. The day has just begun," she said, starting to throw her ass in a circle with her little boy shorts on.

"I know you not tryna battle." I joked, hopping up out of bed.

"Save it for the club, Ivy." she said, and I smacked my lips.

"Oh, so that's what you have planned for tonight, huh? A night out at the club."

"Ugh, you always wanna get things out of me. Bye,"

Jai said, stomping her little feet out the door while I laughed.

I had a feeling this birthday was going to be crazy, like crazier than last year. Last year, things were fairly calm. I had a nice brunch with my family, and then during the night, we did hookah. Rashad took me on a vacation to Jamaica for damn near a week. *Talk about a vibe.* I loved a good turn up, don't get me wrong, but if I could be a homebody, then trust me, I would. Clearly, my job as a bottle girl killed that fantasy because as soon as I got the job, I was outside damn near every day.

Make no mistakes though, when I said fuck Club Wishes, I meant that shit with everything in me. I wasn't going back, and I hadn't been back. Right now, I was looking for something else, maybe another club, but that was hard when my child's father was trying to stop my bag. Since Rashad had his hands in club promotions, he made sure that I wouldn't get a job in any other club, just enacts he didn't want his child's mother in that type of spotlight.

I guess I got that, but at the end of the day, I was a grown ass woman. I had responsibilities and a whole child. He might've expected me to come back crawling to him, but that was out of the question. I remembered those words he said to me at Kordell's welcome home party and how I would need him before he would need me. Rashad wanted to be right so bad with that statement, but I was standing my ground. I'd figure something out. I always did.

Going to the bathroom, I washed my face and brushed my teeth, and then I was headed downstairs. As soon as I hit the stairs, the smell of food hit my nose, and my greedy ass damn near ran down all thirty of them steps.

"Happy birthday, Ivy!" Aniya yelled loudly as she threw some confetti at me.

"You so extra, just like Jai." I laughed and hugged her. "Thank you."

"You're welcome. You want your gift now or later?" she asked as we walked to the kitchen.

"It don't matter. Jai, can we eat now? I'm hungry," I said, fixing my eyes on the many pans that lined across the island. *Was this lunch or dinner?* Jai had everything from meats to sides.

"Okay, it's in the car. I'll be right back," Aniya said walking off.

"Yeah, you can eat now. I think we just waiting on the cornbread," Jai said, handing me a plate. "Oh, I can make your plate. You the birthday girl, right? Have a seat," the chef said, taking the plate out of my hand. He was fairly handsome, light skin with an arm full of tattoos and a fresh line up.

"Oh okay," I said when he smiled, and I peeped his

dimples. He had to be in our age bracket. "Jai, where you find this fine ass chef from?" I whispered to her while I took my seat at the table.

"Girl, he's Kordell's people. Fine, isn't he? I'll slide you his number if you want me to." She laughed, and I rolled my eyes playfully.

"Bye."

"Damn, something sure smells good in here," Sammy said, bursting through the door with Aniya right behind him.

"Oh, for me?" I said excitedly, noticing he had a few Gucci shopping bags in his hands.

"Yeah, you know yo' big cousin gotta come bearing gifts. It's only right. Happy birthday, Ivy," he said, giving me a hug, and I smacked my lips.

"Nigga, you know I'm older than you, but thank you, Sammy. I love you." I hugged him back.

"Man, by four months. How many times I gotta say it?" Sammy said, and I mushed his head. "Get out my face, Sammy."

"Gladly," he said, handing me the gifts and then running over to the food.

Jai and Aniya both were cracking up. "Okay, this is from me, just a little Balenciaga mama," Aniya said, handing me a blue Balenciaga mini bag with the shoes to match.

"Okay now, y'all better spoil y'all big cousin. We love to see it. Thank you, Aniya." I hugged her.

"You're welcome."

"Kordell, went to go pick up my gift for you. He should be back soon," Jai said, sitting next to me at the table.

"Okay cool. Umm… I'll be right back," I said, getting up from the table. Rashad had texted me three times, telling me to come outside. For what, I don't know. I just wanted to be discreet with this mainly because of him and Sammy. I knew neither one of them didn't let shit ride after that ghetto ass fight that broke out.

I hated drama with a passion, so I would try my best to keep the two of them away from each other as much as I could. It would work for the most part, until something came up that had to deal with Kacey… then I didn't know. Hopefully, they'd try to be mature. It was all petty if you asked me.

When I went outside, I spotted Rashad parked down the driveway. He was standing outside of his Tesla with a few pink and silver balloons that read happy birthday. This pop up was very much so unexpected, but when it came to Rashad, he always found a way to be present in my life, someway, somehow.

"What's all of this?" I asked, walking over to him with my arms crossed. I couldn't deny he was looking good in his off-white tee and sneakers, Cartier frames, and gold chains. He even got him a fresh line up that made the curls on the top of his head stick out more. My child's father was fine, but that was all he'd get out of me right now.

"It's yo' birthday, isn't it? I brought Kacey too," he said, opening up the car door.

A smile automatically appeared on my face when I saw my son. He had spent the night with Rashad, but we talked on FaceTime before he went to school this morning.

"Hey, handsome. You look so cute." I ran over to him, taking him out his seat. Lord, he looked just like his daddy. It wasn't even funny. And he was so occupied on his tablet that he barely wanted to give his mama some attention.

"Hey, Mama," he said with his eyes on the screen. Still, he managed to give me a hug and a kiss. "So I was thinking we'd go out for lunch, you know, on some family shit. I know you love you some crab legs," Rashad said as I moved Kacey further up onto my hip.

"I'm already eating with family now, but I'll take Kacey." If I didn't do anything else but spend my birthday with my son, I would be satisfied. I cherished every little moment with him because I knew he couldn't stay my baby forever, and more kids was out of the question.

"That's cool with me. I got something for you though,"

he said, opening up his car door and pulling out a green box. "For you, Ivy," he said, opening the box and revealing a bust down AP. It was beautiful with diamonds all around. I was a female, so of course, my eyes lit up. It was perfect. I gasped and smiled.

"Whatttt! Oh my God! This is big." The excitement was written all over my face, and Rashad saw it. Even he had a smile on his face. I just couldn't tell if it was because he was genuinely happy that I was happy or because he thought he had me right in the palm of his hands.

The second thought made more sense. That was why I was hesitant to take the watch from him. "Wait, Rashad, if I take this watch from you, that means this is a gift for me with no strings attached. I don't owe you anything, nor is it expected for me to be all up on your dick now." I let it be known.

Rashad smacked his lips. "Man, why you always gotta go that route? I bought you this shit off the strength that it's yo' birthday, and you deserve it. Nothing more, nothing less," he said.

Did I believe him though? Fuck no. I started not to even take the watch from him, but I couldn't resist myself.

"Hmm, okay. Well, thank you. I really like it," I said, giving him a hug.

"It's whatever, for my family. You're welcome," he said, kissing my forehead. "Let me see you put it on, baby," he said, taking my hand and placing the watch on my left wrist. "Perfect fit. Oooh, yo' shit dancing, baby. Ain't no light needed," he said, gassing me up, and I couldn't help but smile.

"Stop," I said, pushing him away from me while he laughed.

"Yeah, it look good on you fo' sho. What you got planned for tonight though, Ivy?"

"I don't know. Nothing really until Jai said she had something for me, so I guess that and then after just come back home," I told him, and he nodded his head.

"You ain't got nothing planned for tomorrow though, do you?" he asked.

"Rashad, what you getting at? I know it's something." I knew this man like the back of my hand.

He was up to something for sure. I was trying to be a stiffer ass bitch instead of letting shit slide, so he had to come up with new ways to approach me. Both he and I knew I wasn't going for that same ole, same ole.

"You tryna catch a flight to Cabo or what?" he asked, and I laughed right in his face.

"Goodbye, Rashad. Thank you for the watch. Kacey, tell your daddy bye. You'll see him later."

"Bye, Daddy." Kacey kissed his father while still in my arms.

"Bye, son. So it's like that, Ivy?" Rashad said, looking over to me.

"Boy, it's been like that. You just can't open your eyes to see it. Have a nice day," I said, turning in my tracks.

He could watch my nice, fat ass walk away and cry in the car for all I cared. Going on a trip with Rashad was dead. All he wanted to do was fuck and control me.

I wasn't comfortable with fucking around with Rashad because I knew I wasn't the only woman he was entertaining, and I wanted something real. If it was just about sex for me, then I could've been and fucked on the next nigga. I wanted something permanent. I wanted loyalty, and these days, that was hard to find, so I'd just focus on being the best mother I could be.

"Damn, where you go? I thought I was gonna have to come find you," Jai said when I entered her house.

"Y'all wasn't that damn worried," I said, peeping everybody was eating without me.

"Well, I was hungry as hell and this food 'bout good as hell so.... You better get you a plate," Sammy said as I took a seat at the table with Kacey in my lap.

"You hungry, Kacey?" I asked, and he shook his head

no.

"Oh shit. Don't think I wasn't gon' notice that ice on yo' wrist, Ivy. What the fuck? Now this is birthday energy," Jai said, grabbing my wrist and putting it in the air. "Rashad gave this to you? As he mothafuckin' should," she said, beginning to record a video on her phone.

"He still a pussy ass nigga, if you ask me. I hope he don't expect shit in return either 'cause that's a dub," Sammy said, grabbing my wrist while I snatched away from him.

"Don't disrespect him in front of his son. Thank you. And he already knows what's up with me. I let that be known right then and there before I even took the watch from him," I spoke, purposely leaving out the part of Rashad asking me to go to Cabo with him. They didn't need to know all of that.

Sammy slightly chuckled. "Yeah, let me just shut my ass up."

"Please," Jai said, and Sammy smacked his lips and slightly mushed her head.

Sammy wanted to big brother all of us and being the only boy, he felt like he had a responsibility to look after us, even if Jai and I were older.

"Well, I think you should've told him to keep that watch, as beautiful as it is. We all know how he is. You can hold your own, Ivy, birthday or not. I wouldn't trust it," Aniya said.

"Thank you," Sammy said, cosigning.

"Whatever. Chef, can I have my plate now? Thank you," I said, ready to eat. I was too ready to change the subject. I should've taken the watch off before I even stepped foot inside, but I didn't think it would be such a huge thing. Clearly, I was wrong.

"I got you," the chef said, bringing my plate over.

"Mommy, can I have some?" Kacey said, looking up at me.

"You just said you wasn't hungry, boy," I said as he laughed, and I did the same. "Yes, you can have some, baby." Kacey and I said grace, and then we dug in.

"Auntie Joy didn't call you yet?" Jai asked, and I sighed dramatically.

"No, and it's fine. Before y'all try to make this a big thing as well, how about we just change the subject?"

Was I surprised that my mother had yet to call her daughter and say happy birthday? Hell no. Some years, she did, and some, she didn't. I was tough enough to not charge it to her heart. That was all I'd say about that.

"I don't know what be going through Auntie Joy mind. It's like she's a whole different person these days," Sammy said while I rolled my eyes.

"I'm back," Kordell said, walking through the kitchen.

"Thank God," I mumbled to myself.

"Happy birthday, family. You catching up to the grown folks," he said, giving me a hug.

"Thank you, K."

"This from Jai. This from me," he said, handing me two bags.

"Thank you," I said about to set them down.

"No, no, no, no, open it now. It's some good shit, I promise," Jai said, making me laugh.

"Dang, okay."

Going through the first bag, I saw Jai gifted me two Cartier bracelets. "Okay, big money Jai. Thank you," I said, giving her a hug.

"You know, small things to a giant," Jai said, popping her shit.

"Ooh... a Versace robe? Okay, Killa K. I love it. Thank you," I told Kordell.

"It was nothing to a boss," he said, dusting off his shoulders.

"See now, I see why y'all are together. It all makes sense. The perfect match." I shook my head while everybody laughed.

After everybody finished eating, and as planned, Jai

pampered me with everything I could think of. She even had to squeeze her and Aniya in the mix, but I wasn't mad at that. These were my cousins—sisters.

We finished our self-care around seven, and then we went to look for outfits for tonight. After that, we were pregaming in Jai's living room. Kacey was back with his dad, so I was in the clear to get as drunk as I wanted to get.

"Let's take another shot," Jai said, already pouring a few cups up.

"Another one? We already took four. If y'all want me to make it outside, y'all better slow up, or I'm gonna be passed out in somebody's bed, respectfully," Aniya said, tapping out.

"I'll take one more with you, Jai, and then that's a wrap. We off of 1942 too? Oh yeah, you showing out," I said, grabbing the red plastic cup and downing my shot.

"No chaser, no chaser, Ivy," Jai said, taking my lemonade from my hand.

"Just for that, I'm not drinking no more tonight," I said, grabbing my purse and phone.

"Yes the fuck you are. I'm gonna get you so drunk that you gon' forget how to spell your name, and it's only three letters," Jai said, and my mouth dropped.

"Oh hell no. Take me home," Aniya said, heading for the door.

"No, ma'am. We in this together," I said, grabbing her hand.

"Let's all go," I let it be known.

"You know I got us a driver. Ain't no way I'm driving—none of us for that matter," Jai said, locking her front door.

While we all stood there, I took a moment to take in how good we looked. Jai wore a Versace two-piece pants and bra set with a pair of Versace black and gold heels. Her hair was bone straight in a ponytail going all the way to her ass. She wore a red lip with a light beat and a nice AP on her wrist just like mine. Not to mention, she had a nice diamond ring on her finger, but she swore it wasn't an engagement, because she'd tell us.

Aniya wore a pair of leather black pants that hugged her small frame just right with a red and black Chanel top that revealed her breasts somewhat. On her feet, she wore a pair of Christian Louboutin heels with the red at the bottom. Her hair was in a middle-part bob, and just like Jai she had the natural beat going on, but instead of a red lip, she did some gloss. On her wrist, she wore a diamond tennis bracelet that her boyfriend gifted her. Her red Chanel bag really brought it out.

I wore a two-piece Christian Dior black and pink short set with a pair of black Tom Ford heels. I switched from loose wave to deep wave hair, twenty-eight inches to be exact. On my wrist, I rocked the brand-new AP Rashad gifted me along with the Cartier bracelet from Jai. I never went for the glamorous look, so my makeup was fairly natural. I carried a small black Chanel bag that matched with the diamond Chanel earrings in my ear.

I'd say my family and I looked damn good, but that was on a regular.

After we took a few pictures and videos of each other, together we were off. To where, I didn't know. Jai just said the club, and I was cool with that as long as it wasn't Club Wishes. That would've ruined my whole mood. Luckily, Jai had something better in mind—Liv.

As soon as we walked in the club, it was a movie. I didn't know how the scene was on a Friday night, but tonight, it was what it should be. We had our own section of course, so that was the first place we were escorted by security. Jai managed to arrange cutouts of my name for the bottle girls to hold. She even decorated our section with balloons and all of my favorite drinks.

"Jai, I had no idea you was gonna go this hard for me," I said, giving her a hug.

"It's your Kobe year. It's up. Happy birthday, bitch," she said, recording me while I did me a quick spin for her and started to shake a little something for the camera. The whole time, Jai gassed me up. "Let's take a shot," she said, grabbing a bottle of Hennessy.

"No, ma'am. You not finna have me mixing liquor and wanting to fight in this bitch." I quickly shut her down. "Pass me what I've been drinking on all night, 1942." I said, taking a seat on the small couch.

"I got you. Be right back," she said. leaving me and Aniya in the section.

"Here come yo' big-headed cousin," Aniya said, pointing out Sammy coming over with a few of his friends.

"Know he gon' be talking shit all night." I laughed to myself.

Sammy was protective of us on a regular, but when we went out, it was a whole other different story. He was worse than the damn CIA. At all times, he had to know what we were doing and who we were with.

"Yeah, he gon' be getting on your nerves 'cause I definitely invited my man out. He should be here in a few," Aniya said while I smacked my lips.

"Y'all bitches really finna be boo'd up while I'm in here single as the fuck? Yeah, I'm definitely getting drunk. Fuck y'all."

Kordell was definitely pulling up as well, so I knew

what that meant. Jai and Aniya were going to be all in their men's faces while I was left to have fun by myself.

That just wasn't going to fly today. Jai pulled me out of the crib to celebrate on her, so that meant it would be no hugging up with your nigga. Tonight, we would be taking shots, making memories, and genuinely having a good time. Period.

"We're not gonna be boo'd up, trust me. I know how to have a good time while Kamal is around," Aniya said while I rolled my eyes.

"Mhm, we gon' see."

"What's up! What's up! What's up!" Sammy said fully in our presence. "Nah, Ivy, you showing too much. You too, Aniya. Make me get my belt," he said, about to take his jean jacket off and put it on me.

"Stop. Don't start that shit, Sammy. I'm not playing," I told him while his friends laughed.

"I'm back!" Jai said excitedly with a few bottle girls behind her carrying multiple bottles of 1942.

Was it too early to tap out? Because that was the way I was feeling. Out of all of us, Jai's alcohol tolerance was the best. I didn't think I'd ever seen her extremely drunk before, and that girl can drink for real.

"Take a shot, Ivy," Jai said, pouring me up.

"I just took one." I pouted.

"Take another one then," Jai said, more so telling than asking.

"Stop peer pressuring. This is not the fuckin' ninth grade," Sammy said, taking my shot for me. He was good for something.

"You not off the hook, Ivy," Jai said as the bottle girls put all our drinks down.

"Yeah, whatever. Dance with me," I said, putting her drink down.

The DJ had been playing all the good songs tonight, so imagine how I felt when that classic Trina came on. Being from the 305, all her shit was an anthem, and I wasn't trying to do any talking. All I expected to see was ass shaking in the air, and that was just that on that.

"You ain't gotta tell me twice," Jai said, kicking off her heels, and I did the same.

Right when the beat dropped, so did our asses. We did that shit with no effort. We had to know how to put on a show being from Miami. Dancing just came natural since I was seven if I was being honest.

Jai and I held on to each other while we shook our asses with not a care in this world. Aniya recoded us the whole time while everybody's eyes were on us—in the section or not. We were just a vibe.

"Okay, that's enough. See? This why I don't like going out with y'all. Y'all always feel like y'all gotta shake some ass. How about a little two-step or something? Shit, I'll even take a little lean with it, rock with it. Sit down," Sammy said, gently pushing us both into a seat.

"Nigga, I'm yo' big sister. You must've forgot. Find you somebody to play with," Jai said, getting right back up and starting to twerk once again.

"Alright, that's enough of that shit," Kordell said, coming out of nowhere.

"Yeah, let me see you talk that shit with him since you bad," Sammy said, instigating, and Jai smacked her lips.

"Boy, shut up. My nigga know how I am. Trust," Jai said, throwing it back on Kordell.

I lived. I loved her.

"How much you have to drink, Jai?" Kordell said, sitting her in his lap.

"Just two shots, babe," she casually spoke.

"Times ten." I laughed with Jai.

Kordell shook his head. "No more drinking tonight. Not until you take a pregnancy test," he said, and I started to feel bad like I was his girl or something.

"Umm... Jai, come to the bathroom with me please," I

said, standing up and grabbing her hand.

"Of course, I'll be back, baby," she told Kordell as we walked hand in hand out of the section. "Now you know…" I trailed off as she sighed.

"Please don't make me feel worse than I already do. You wanna see me crying? I got enough liquor in my system," she said as I remained silent.

There was no need to say another word because she knew how I felt about the situation. She needed to have a conversation with him. I said it twice, and I'd say it again.

After going to the bathroom, Jai and I made a few drunk video and pictures, and then we returned to our section. There were a few more people present this time, but I recognized them to be Kordell's people, so I wasn't really tripping. Looking to the left of me, I saw Kamal was finally here, and Aniya was loving every second of it.

I sighed. Both of my cousins were going home to get dick, and it wasn't either of their birthdays. Tragic. I wouldn't dare call Rashad, even though I knew he'd be down. I wasn't even drunk enough for all of that.

"Take a shot if you love yourself. It's a celebration toast," Sammy said, passing not one but two shots to everybody.

"Fuck it. It's my birthday," I said, downing both of

them. Between the constant shots and contact high I was catching, I felt too damn good. The night just kept going, and I was having so much fun with my people.

"Bitch, you better shake the room!" Aniya shouted as soon as Pop Smoke came on.

This song always put me in a mood, and I was already feeling damn good. Gladly handing her my cup, I did just that while she and Jai both threw stacks of twenties on me as if I were a dancer. I couldn't help but laugh.

I always felt eyes on me heavy whenever I was on the scene, but this time, it just felt different. Through all those flashes on me from the camera, I still spotted not just Ty, but Breeze and Rodney as well. The three of them stood there peeping the scene. Ty, on the other hand was focused on me or should I say my body. Maybe the drinks were way too strong because there was no way I just kept running into Ty. I didn't believe in coincidences, so what was really up?

"Kordell, you didn't invite them?—Breeze at that." Aniya pouted, pulling him to the side.

"Yeah, Ty my nigga. I ran into him at his spot yesterday and told him to come through. What's the problem?" Kordell said all clueless.

"You got her ex nigga and her current nigga in the same spot. What you expect?" I said, and Kordell's face went blank before he laughed some.

"Oh, damn. I ain't even know. My bad, Aniya," he said as I started to crack up.

I was sorry. I just couldn't help it. It was the fact Kordell really didn't know.

Aniya smacked her lips. "Yeah, yeah, yeah. We're leaving, bye. Happy birthday, Ivy," she said, giving me a hug and then going over to Kamal.

We all exchanged a few more words with each other, and then, just like Aniya said, she and Kamal were leaving. The whole time, I watched Breeze stare at them. I felt he was about to approach them until Rodney pulled him back. Good. We didn't need the drama.

"Where did Aniya go?" Jai said as I sat next to her.

I didn't even have to say a word I just moved her head in the direction of Breeze, and she caught on.

"Oops, damn." She laughed just like Kordell. "Anyways, you gon' take another shot?" Jai said as I hid my face in my hands.

"Leave me alone, Jainice," I said, literally getting up and running from her. Of course she followed me.

"Come on, Ivy. Don't be like that." She laughed, grabbing my head and pouring the shot down my throat herself.

"Bitch, no more. I can barely stand," I said, falling right into Ty's lap.

He was having a full-blown conversation with Kordell, yet he was there to catch me—all of me at that.

"Oh shit—my bad." I began to get up, but Ty held my hips in a tight, firm grip.

"Nah, you good. I heard it's your birthday," he said, and I turned to face him.

"You heard right."

Facing him, I took the time to observe him closely. As always, he was looking and smelling good. In just a plain, white tee and a few diamond chains on, he had me doing a little contemplating. The club was noisy as hell, but I found myself getting lost in his brown eyes. His mouth continued to move, but I wasn't focused on his words, just his lips. They looked so soft. I'd admit, he had me caught up. I felt he knew that too, which was why he just smiled.

"I'm sorry. What were you saying?"

"Happy birthday, shorty." He smirked, and I laughed a little.

"Thank you, Ty," I said, trying to get up for a second time, but just like before, he had this tight grip on me. Not wanting to argue him down, I turned back around and continued to enjoy my night. Crazy thing was we sat like this the whole time like it was normal for us or something. Weird.

"If you wanna dance, then dance. I ain't gon' stop you," Ty said, tapping my thigh.

I guess he noticed me moving around on him a little bit. I tried my hardest not to move around, but the DJ was playing the City Girls. How was I supposed to be still in my seat? How?

"I bet you won't," I said, giving him a quick glance as he smirked.

"Umm… is there something you wanna tell me?" Jai said, pulling me close to her.

"Not at all."

"Mhm, can we get some more shots going for the people new to the party?" Jai stood.

"Nah, I definitely tap out." I shook my head. If I took one more drink, somebody would have to carry me out of here. That was another reason why I stayed in Ty's lap. A bitch could barely move.

"What you tapping out for? It's your day," Ty said.

"Nigga, you ain't been here all night like I have. I quit. Take me out the game, coach," I spoke seriously while he laughed.

"Just one more… with me."

"Don't be giving me that nice smile of yours, tryna win

me over, Ty. I'm good… Okay, fine, just one more." I smiled, taking that shot down just like the others. As soon as the warm liquor hit my throat, I regretted it. The night was about to get real interesting.

"One time for the birthday bitch! Two times for the birthday bitch!" Jai screamed, hyping me up like she did all night.

It was only right I did me before we called it a night. Still in Ty's lap, I started to wind my hips in a circular motion, going with the beat. Grabbing my thighs, I slightly stood, shaking my ass. The whole time, Rodney watched me with a creepy ass look on his face. I didn't like him, and I didn't want to. When I caught his stares, I rolled my eyes at him, and he smiled at me.

"You keep grinding on my shit like that, you gon' have to see about me," Ty said with his raspy voice in my ear, sending a single chill down my spine.

"I tried to get up. If you can't handle me, then just say that," I said as he shot me a challenging look. Cocky Ty was about to make his grand entrance. His face told me just that.

"So let's see about it then." He shrugged. "You the one who seem unsure. I'm well aware of what I can do… or what I know how to do for that matter," he said, placing both of his hands on my thighs. The only thing I felt was moist.

Not knowing what to say, I laughed his remarks off, even though I knew, for a fact, Ty wasn't playing any games with my drunk ass.

"Let's slide. I ain't tryna be here when all these people clear out," Kordell said, and I fully agreed.

I needed to sleep everything off. Barely able to stand, Ty took my hand.

"Wait, give me a minute," I said, stopping in my tracks. It was like as soon as I stood up, all the liquor I encountered rushed from my head to my toes.

"Yeah, she fucked up. It's written all over her face." Breeze laughed while Ty grabbed my hand and tried his best to lead me outside.

"Pick me up, Ty," I told him while I grabbed my heels from the ground.

"I got you," he said, picking me up bridal style and carrying me outside.

"I got your gifts," Sammy said from behind me.

"Mhm," I said softly, tired and barely able to speak. When we got outside, I put all my things in Kordell's car, and that was the last thing I really remembered.

"You good, Ivy?" Ty said, putting me down. He rested his hands on my small waist to help me stand.

"Mhm, take me home."

The rest of the night was a blur from right there. I couldn't even tell you how I got back to Jai and Kordell's house. All I knew was the night ended with me in the back of Ty's Lambo truck under the stars getting ate out. I only remembered that because the head was so damn pleasurable. No female could forget some tongue like that, simply because it was just way too good. From my legs shaking to the constant moans, I remembered it all.

Whenever I ran into him again, because I was sure I would again. I'd most definitely, try to forget this night. Who the fuck was I kidding? Ty was unforgettable in every aspect.

Fuck.

# *Kordell*

"Appreciate it," I told the cashier at the floral shop as he handed me my receipt. I was getting Jai some flowers along with some other surprises. Things had been good with me and her. We just hadn't been communicating about the important things in life, like work, partnership, and of course kids.

I loved Jai with everything in me. I wanted her to be the mother of my kids since the beginning. Sometimes it surprised me that we didn't have a few by now. If I wouldn't have did that that time, there would be plenty little us running around, but timing was everything.

After thinking long and hard, I decided to just let all that street shit ride. That part of my life wasn't needed now, not if I wanted to put my focus on my family strictly. It was different back then. Before, I would run the streets nonstop while I stacked all the bread I could up. Jai and I were together completely. Shit, I even had her on the block with me a few times. That was how cool our relationship was.

Thinking about now and the future, I just wanted different. She could go into any business that she wanted to, and I would support her, or if she chose to be a stay-at-home mother, that was also cool with me. I just wanted things between us to be well established. There was no doubt in my mind that she wanted the same thing either. She loved me, she was solid, and she was going to stay down. That was good enough for me.

I planned to shower her with gifts and show my appreciation for her today. I was an affectionate nigga all around, and I always did things for her just because I loved her. However, today was personal. It was me showing my gratitude to Jai for being a real ass female and holding me down. Many bitches in her shoes would've folded under pressure, but she stood ten toes down for her nigga, and for that reason, she could get anything for me.

It was going on 5:30 in the afternoon, and I had to get back to the crib before she did to make sure everything was set up right. I didn't want to go out to dinner or outside at all. The crib was perfect for a romantic night, plus when I was ready to slide in my girl, I wouldn't have to wait. I was a nigga that could make a way out of anything. Our living room was about to look like a fairy tale fucking with me.

When I got back to the crib, I immediately started setting up the living room with rose petals, balloons, candles, fruit, and champagne. Jai was the nosy type, so I was in a rush. She and Ivy were out shopping, so I figured I had a little time. Jai was going to spend a bag on designer stuff for sure. It was all good though because she deserved it.

Things were looking perfect. I had a chef whipping up her favorite foods, I had a massage set up for her, and I even ran her a hot bath. I was going all out for her, and the night hadn't even started yet. I had so many tricks up my sleeve for my baby. I just knew she would love it.

Pulling out my ringing phone from my pocket, I saw it was Jai. "What's up, baby?" I answered. "What you doing? You want me to bring you something to eat back since I'm already out?" she asked as I looked over to the chef who was just about done cooking.

"Nah, I'm good. I already ate." I lied, trying to keep things a secret until she got here.

"You sure, Kordell? I'm telling you now, I'm not cooking when I get home," Jai said, and I laughed.

She was always like this—caring and concerned to say the least. I bet I if I told her no, she'd still call me back ten minutes later asking me the same exact question. That was just how she was, but tonight, it was my job to be caring and take care of her—mentally, physically, and emotionally. Nothing else mattered at this given moment but her.

"Yeah, Jai. I'm good. Where you at anyways?" I said, grabbing a few of her gifts and hiding them in our closet.

"On my way home in a few. Me and Ivy are still shopping. I got you a few things too, babe. You're gonna love it," she said as I got quiet and started to think.

I was always a good judge of character when it came to anybody, so yeah, I did pay attention to the little things, like how Jai always thought about me in damn near everything she did. That was love. I was the same way, especially in the beginning. I was so in love. Jai had me buying flowers like twice a week. I didn't even want to leave the crib half of the time, and I loved the hustle. Shit, that should tell enough. My love ran deep for her.

"You hear me, Kordell?" Jai said, taking me out of my thoughts.

"Yeah, I hear you. You ain't have to get me anything though," I told her while she smacked her lips.

"If I wanna splurge on my nigga, then I will."

"Well, excuse me," I replied in a sarcastic tone.

"I'm not about to play with you. I'll see you soon. I love you."

"I love you too," I said, hanging up.

While Jai was still out, I decided to take a quick shower and make sure I was good myself. I stopped by Sammy's spot earlier so he could get me right with the clippers, and as expected, he did just that. I wasn't too fond to be sitting in any nigga's chair because I valued my hairline and beard way too much. Being away for five years would have anyone damn skeptical, even them niggas inside knew what it was with me when it came to that perfect cut. I didn't play that shit.

After I jumped out the shower, I got dressed in a pair of Amiri jeans and a single white tee. Jai had sent me a text saying she was five minutes away, so I planned to greet her at the door. Spraying on some Gucci cologne, I jogged down the stairs with a dozen red roses in my hand.

"Kordell, why do you have both locks locked?" Jai said, starting to bang on the door loudly. She probably thought it was some bullshit going on. Little did she know she was way off.

"Stop banging on my door like that," I said, unlocking and opening up the front door while she mugged the fuck outta me.

"Stop playing with me," she said, pushing me out of the way while she dropped her bags at the door. She was so caught up on being a woman that she didn't even notice all the beautiful things I had set up for her. "I smell food. Did you cook? All this for me?" She gasped and turned in her tracks. There was that smile that I adored so much. "Aww, baby," she said, running straight to me and jumping into my arms.

"You ain't even seen nothing yet." I slightly laughed while she continued to hold on to me for dear life.

"Show me then," she said, kissing my lips twice and

letting me go.

I smacked her ass. "Follow me," I said, leading the way to the living room.

"My favorite candles… you remembered. It's so beautiful, K. Don't make me cry," she said, kicking off her red bottoms and picking up some of the flowers from the couch. "I can't believe you did this," she said, pulling me down to the ground and sitting on my lap. Her hands went straight to my zipper, but before things could go further, I stopped her.

"We gon' get to that for sure, but first, there's more you need to see," I told her as she sighed. "All I wanna see is you pushing inside of me."

"I turned you into a monster." I laughed and tapped her leg. "Get up," I said, and she did so. "What you wanna do first? I got you a warm bath going, some food, and massage, plus gifts," I told her while she smiled and started to think.

"Bath first. massage, food, then gifts," she said, and I nodded.

"Bet, go upstairs and get out your clothes. I'll be right there."

"Don't be all day. I want you to get in with me."

"I just got out the shower. It's all about you. I'll be up there to rub your feet though," I told her. "Kordell, I'm snatching your soul tonight, I swear. You just don't even know," she said, eyeing me up and down with a lustful expression on her face.

If I didn't have all these people in my crib right now, I'd probably say fuck it and get straight to the fun part. I could be a gentleman though. That was never a problem for me.

"Do what you gotta do, Jai." I joked.

"Hurry, baby." She started to walk up the stairs.

"I'm right behind you," I said, first going into the kitchen. Everything was set up nicely from dinner to dessert. "Aye, you can start putting the food out in about twenty minutes. We should be down then," I told the chef, and he agreed. I peeped the steak, lobster, mashed potatoes, shrimp, and so on. My girl could eat and knew her way around the kitchen, so I already knew this food was going to put another smile on her face.

Grabbing a bottle of champagne and the fruit tray from the living room, I walked upstairs to our bedroom.

"Come on, Kordell," Jai shouted from inside the tub.

I barely even made a sound, yet she knew I was there. That was how it always was. It was like she could feel my presence or something. I always thought it was crazy or weird, but then she'd just tell me I was a part of her soul. "Patience, Jainice," I said, setting the fruit and champagne on the bed.

Going into our closet, I started to pull some of her gifts

out. I was able to hide the gifts perfectly, making sure they were either blended in and not noticeable. Her favorite designer brand was Louis Vuitton, so that was where most of her gifts came from. I bought her a purse, wallet, sandals, and scarf with some off-white luggage. When I said I had tricks up my sleeve, I meant that. Soon, me and my shorty would be taking trips—sandy beaches, warm weather, and clear water. *Yeah, that sounded like a vibe.*

After bringing the gifts onto the bed, I realized I forgot her Dior anklet. Reaching for the top shelf to grab the small bag, a clear bin of paper came crashing down on me, hitting a nigga right in his head. "Fuck," I said to myself as I gathered the papers from the ground and put them away. Stopping in my tracks I ran across a few papers that were stapled together.

Looking at the top of the thick packet I saw it was from a women's doctor, and a few things were highlighted. Reading over the paperwork, I assumed it was some normal shit, considering Jai's height and weight was on here, but as I continued to work my way down, I couldn't believe my eyes.

Jai was on fucking birth control for weeks and didn't tell me shit.

Grabbing the piece of paper, I stormed out of the closet. All I saw was red. All I felt was anger.

"Finall—"

"You think I'm fucking stupid? What kind of nigga you think you fucking with?" I yelled, pulling Jai's naked body out of the tub and pushing her against the wall.

"What the fuck is wrong with you?" she cried, confused and slightly trembling.

"What the fuck is wrong with you? You thought I wouldn't find out?" I held the paper up to her.

She didn't even have to look at it longer than five seconds because she knew. Her grimy ass knew she fucked up.

"I was—"

"Fuck you, Jai! Don't say another mothafuckin' word to me!" I pushed her to the side and walked off. I wanted to strangle this damn girl with my bare hands for moving the way she did. I knew how bad my anger could get, so before I did something I would regret, it was best that I left the crib.

Sliding on my shoes, I grabbed my phone and car keys.

"Can we please talk, Kordell. I'm sorry. I should've told you—I was gonna tell you. It just never seemed like the right time," Jai said, coming out of the restroom with a robe on. I couldn't even look at her because all I saw was somebody I didn't recognize. There was just so many things going on in my mind, and all the greatness that we were was nowhere in my thoughts. This was the lowest shit she had ever done to me. Fuck it. I was hurt as a man—as her man.

"You grimy. I see you for who you really are. Ain't no way my bitch would keep something like that from me. Whole time, I'm thinking we building, and you moving funny like this! I cannot fuckin' trust you!" I barked, approaching her, making her jump.

"Please, just let me tell you why. I never meant to hurt you. You know the love I have for you is real. I was just scared," she said while I smacked my lips.

"Here you go again with this scared shit. Stop using excuses! Be a fuckin' woman! Dawg, I can't even look at you right now on everything. You fuckin' scandalous, and you know it." I pointed my finger in her face.

"I was scared. When I asked you if you were done with that life, I knew you lied. You were still thinking about it. I didn't want to have to raise a child in this lifestyle, K," she cried. "I want something better—marriage, kids, and a happily ever after. Nothing half ass, so if birth control was the only thing that stopped me from getting hurt, then so be it." She sniffled and crossed her arms.

This couldn't be my reality right now. There was no way in hell Jainice was giving me these lame ass answers. She wasn't even remorseful, and that was what pissed me off the most about the whole situation. If I wouldn't have found those papers, I would still be walking around this bitch thinking there was hope for a child right now. She didn't give a fuck about me or my feelings, because she was too busy protecting hers. *Wow, man, it's a cold, cold world out here.*

"You selfish ass female. I'm gone." I shook my head, turning away from her before things got worse.

"Please don't go, Kordell," she said, pulling on my arm.

"Jai let me the fuck go before I lay yo' ass out for real." I warned her while she still held on to me tightly.

"No, I'm not letting you go. We're supposed to be better than this," she had the nerve to say.

"And see, that's what I thought! Not once did you come to yo' nigga and tell me how you really felt!" I said, yanking away from her, making her hit the ground. "All yo' disloyal ass had to do was ask me—all you had to do, Jai, and I would've told you. I'd give up that shit in a heartbeat for you and my child, but yo' childish ass wanna play games like we kids. I was tryna make a future with yo' simpleminded ass. Now I don't even want anything with you," I spoke, looking directly in her eyes.

That last statement hit hard for her. She looked devastated when those words came out of my mouth, but I was broken too.

"You don't mean that. I know you don't. I know that for a fact. Hurt people, hurt people." She shook her head.

Slightly laughing, I spoke up. "I don't?" Being hurt wasn't at the top of my list right now. It was betrayal. I knew what I said to her, and I meant that shit. I was going to stand on that shit, matter of fact. "Fuck I'ma do with a sneaky ass broad who can't keep it a stack with her man? If that's the case, I might as well go fuck on the next bitch, right? I can get pussy from anywhere, I need loyalty. I expected more from yo' ass. Fuck outta my face, Jai. It's a wrap, and I mean that shit," I said, leaving her on the ground.

It was fuck her for right now. My heart and damn sure my head wouldn't allow me to feel anything but hatred. There was nothing else to be said at this point. She meant for her actions to play out the way she did because she actually allowed herself to do some stupid shit like that to me out of all people. I mean, how else did she think this shit would play out? I didn't know. What I did know was I was over this whole family thing. I let being in love stop me from being who I truly was—a hustling, get money ass nigga. I was ready to get back to me.

Pulling out my phone, I hit Ty up. "I'm ready to work. Whatever you need me for, I'm with it, nigga."

"So what can I do for you, Ty?" Montell said, sitting on the opposite side of his desk. I didn't even want to be in this bitch because it smelled horrible, reeking of sex. With all the bitches he was running through here like it was nothing, I'd think his ass would have the courtesy to make sure his office was clean and smelling good.

The women here at Club Wishes really had low self-esteem and it showed. Montell couldn't offer these girls shit but some extra hours, and he didn't mind giving them out, because that put more money in his pocket. This game was something else. That was why it was a must you learned it. Nobody heard me though.

"You can't do a damn thing for me, Montell, however, I could do a lot for you." Many didn't know me and Montell went way back. Growing up, all the older cats hung around him because he knew his way around the city. He knew the right people and the right connections. That was how we crossed paths.

About five years ago, Montell had this bad gambling habit. He lost his house, car, and sold all his belongings, but he was still about $35,000 short. That was where I came in. I fronted him the cash, not because I had it, but because I sensed an opportunity that could make me back what I gave away in my sleep—Club Wishes.

I had a share in the club. It was a 60/40 split—me getting majority of course. Montell had the experience, and I had the bank. It was a perfect. It was true, many didn't know I had my share in the club because that was the way I wanted it. He could be the face, promote, and keep shit in order while I collected. However, we did have ties. Shit, I even put some of the women on in here. It was just that I didn't have to fuck them to put them in position, even when they threw it at me. Montell, on the other hand, just couldn't say no.

He nervously chuckled and rubbed his chin. "Right, right, so to what do I owe the pleasure? I know you a busy man and all."

"That I am. I just wanted to inform you it's gonna be a slight change around here," I said, and he shot me a surprising look.

"What kind of change we talking? I'm running Club Wishes just the way it's supposed to be ran. Hell, the numbers speak for themselves."

"You doing your job, Montell. I'll hand it to you. Can't say I didn't have my doubts, you know why." I shrugged, and he nodded.

"Yeah, but I'm a different man now. No more

gambling and drinking nonstop, just working," he said, and I laughed right in his face.

"Nigga, you ain't gon' ever change. You got a new hustle, sure, and you might've cut down time on the bottle, but deep inside, you still the same, and you know it. That's beside the point though. What's important is change."

"I'm listening."

"I'll be working more closely here starting next week. There's been a change of plans in my other line of business, so I'll be cleaning money at Club Wishes from now on," I said, getting right to it.

When I told Breeze and Rodney I had a plan, I meant it. Cleaning drug money through the club was the perfect idea. We were making more here than the alley and hair salon, and like I said before, nobody really knew I was a part of something so big. I didn't know if this change would be permanent just yet, but for now it would do.

"But you never wanted anything to do with the club, remember? As long as I paid you your cut, you were good," Montell said.

But that was then, and this is now. If I was cleaning money in here, best believe I would be around way more. I didn't only have one business to look out for. I had two. Money was never anything to play with on my end. If anybody would be the one calling shots and being present it would be me. I couldn't take any chances.

Before, I would only show my face around here maybe twice a month just to see what was up. Sometimes I even came to catch a vibe with my niggas just because this was the spot. Montell would manage the place, keep the women in line, and keep everybody happy while he ran me my cut. Those same rules would apply. It was just now I'd have more say-so then before. If he played his cards right, he'd still be able to make plays. All he had to do was stay out of my way.

"I just told you what it was. You gon' fall in line or what? It's your call. It's your loss if anything." I assured him.

"I just wanna make sure we keep everything the way it is. We got a good thing going here, Ty."

"You think I don't know that? I ain't ever steer you wrong. This is my business too. I know what the fuck I'm doing." Nothing bothered me more than having to repeat myself. I was getting tired just keeping the conversation going honestly. I said what I said, and we'd be moving forward in the direction I wanted to, simple.

Montell sighed and shook his head. "Alright. Whatever you wanna do, I'll fall in line," he said as I expected him to.

"Coo'. I'll let you know when the money starts rolling in," I stood, running my hand through my waves.

"I assume we'll be being very discreet. Things got a little hot when you decided to off a nigga right on the side of my building," Montell said making me turn in my tracks. "I mean, our building," he said, quickly changing up his statement.

He was referring to Mikey. He was the one to get rid of the footage. Rodney made sure of it. He knew what had to be done because if I went down, then so did he. That was never going to happen though. My problem with Montell was he'd sometimes let this place get to him—the attention, money, women, alcohol, and authority. There was so much shit I let him slide with in the past, but things around here were going to be changing more than he knew.

"I'm always discreet. You, on the other hand, not so much." I shook my head and walked up on him. "Shall we discuss the liquor supply shortage that occurs every month because you make Bri bring your bottles from the back to your office? Or the fact you promising bitches extra hours for half of the pay? Or..." I trailed off tapping my head. "How you went raw dogging in the bottle girl Gabby, got her pregnant, threatened her to get an abortion that you made her pay for herself just to demote her to a lower level to teach her a lesson. Now, I told you, Montell, you the same nigga." I chuckled and stepped back.

"Anything else?" he said, clearly ashamed and confused.

This was my business, which was what he failed to realize. I knew everything that went down around here, even the shit he tried to sweep under the rug. I knew.

"Actually, there is…" I said, pulling out my phone and shooting a quick text. Although I said I'd be around more, I was still a busy ass nigga with a lot on my plate. There was no way I could be at more than one place at once. That was where help came in, where she came in. A minute or so passed, and in walked a soul I couldn't escape.

Ivy.

"What the hell is she doing here? She quit on me." Montell stood from his sit angrily.

"Sit yo' ass down for you have a heart attack." I smacked my lips and looked over to Ivy. "Come in," I said, grabbing her hand.

She looked apprehensive and quite fragile. If she didn't know I wouldn't hurt her by now, then I just didn't know.

"What's going on, Ty?" Ivy quietly spoke with her head down. She had no idea what was about to take place.

She didn't know me well enough. Still, she'd be crazy as hell if she passed up on this great opportunity. I was putting money in her pocket, and she barely had to lift a finger.

"Well, I was just about to tell Montell that we just reached a third party in the club. You," I said, pointing at her as her eyes grew wide, and she let my hand go.

"What? No—I-I don't want anything to do with this club or his disgusting ass. What the fuck is this about? I want no parts," she said, about to walk away until I grabbed her by the waist.

"Well, she said it herself, Ty. Nothing we can do now." Montell shrugged his shoulders.

"Aye, give us a minute." I thought maybe I should've talked to Ivy alone in the first place.

"You want me to give y'all a minute in my office?" he asked like it was a problem.

"Nigga, you heard me. I ain't stutter in this bitch. Slide," I commanded him while I still held on to Ivy's small waist.

Montell sighed and did just that. "I'll be right outside." he said, shooting me and then Ivy a look.

I could tell she hated him with a passion, but she didn't have anything to worry about. I had it all under control.

As soon as the door shut, Ivy moved away from me. "I know things have been weird between us, but this has to take the cake. Why me? Ty, I didn't even know you had dealings with the club, and here you are asking me to be a part of something. Why?" Ivy asked. Her reaction was expected, and I planned to give her the rundown, making sure I said just enough but not too much.

"Why not you? You needa job, right?" I smirked, and she rolled her eyes.

"Nigga, don't try and play me. I'm good even when I'm not," she said with an attitude.

"Look, my bad. It's not even like that. I'm just tryna put you in a position to make some money. What's wrong with that?"

"I don't know you, that's what's wrong. Ain't no telling what you wrapped up in, Ty, and I honestly don't need the drama or the problems." She crossed her arms.

I sighed and approached her slowly. She only let me get so close to her though before she put her hand between us. "I ain't gon' lead you wrong. Trust me, Ivy," I said, removing her hand from my chest and bringing her body close to me. "You trust me?" I lifted her chin up so that she was staring me in my eyes.

"No," she said with no hesitation.

It made me laugh because I knew she was lying. Backing her into Montell's desk, I lifted her up, making her sit. "I'ma ask you again. You trust me, Ivy?" I asked for the second time as I rested my left hand on her thigh.

"Yes, I do. For some stupid ass reason, I do, Ty. Happy?" she said, pushing me back some, but I didn't go too far.

"You the one who should be happy for finally accepting the truth," I said while she squinted her eyes at me and then looked away.

"I don't know what you're talking about."

"Alright, you wanna play that game? Coo'. I know the real. I know you remember how I made you feel. What I did to yo body in the back seat of my whip. How you managed to scratch my back up while you smothered me in between yo' thick thighs."

"Ty, shut up, damn," she said, jumping down from the desk and trying to cover my mouth.

"I thought you forgot." I laughed, grabbing both of her hands so she couldn't grab me.

"I wish I did. I don't even know how... You know what? It was the liquor."

That was the perfect excuse. If all else failed, blame it on the alcohol. I knew that rule. Ivy had been drinking that whole night, and she was out of it, but the look in her eyes while we did what we did I could never forget. That look let me know that she was aware of what was taking place. She remembered that night. How the fuck could she forget when dealing with a nigga like me?

"The liquor might've put you in a mood, but it was *you* who wanted *me* to put tongue on you. It's coo'. I enjoyed it." I threw her a smile while she tried to hide hers.

"Anyways, what could you possibly need my help for around here?" Ivy said, changing the subject. I knew all about that.

I was going to let her slide though. We could talk business. I was always up for that. "Just to make sure things running smoothly around here. Of course I'll be in attendance some days, but I do have other responsibilities. I need you to keep me posted on any and everything. Make sure the girls in line. Can you do that for me?" I asked, pulling her by the belt loop of her little ass denim shorts she wore.

She was on some real chill shit with her graphic tee and bun and baby hairs. I couldn't spot an ounce of makeup on her, just lip gloss and lashes. Still she had me ready to run her down right here. There was just something about Ivy that had me intrigued. I was feeling her.

"If I say yes," she said, removing my finger from her shorts, "there's a few things that I ask of you and the rest of the people working here."

"Go 'head." I instructed her.

"Well, first things first, I wanna be respected by

everyone here. Just because I used to work here doesn't mean people can run over me. Secondly, I don't want to have to answer to Montell. I don't even wanna speak to him. I'll need my own space where I can feel like I'm a part of this, so you'll have to make a way. And lastly, you have to have to respect my privacy. All this touching on me has to stop. We clear?"

I couldn't even front and say it wasn't a turn-on to see her take control and demand all these things. A woman in power was just as big as a man in power. I respected it. Her drive let me know that my decision in bringing her along was the right one. Ivy was a different breed. I fucked with it.

"Yeah to all of that. And I won't touch you unless you ask me too. Anything else?" I smirked as she rolled her eyes.

"Yeah, payment. I needa be making more than I was putting up in here, and that was a lot," she said as I nodded my head.

"Ten thousand every other week," I suggested, testing her of course. Even I knew she wouldn't be down with that offer.

Ivy scoffed. "Nigga, what? Who do you think you dealing with," she said, walking up on me. "Listen to me loud and clear, we'll do $50,000 every week, a office space, good parking, and I get to wear whatever I want. Take it or leave it. Either way, I'm good."

"Damn, you tough. You got it though." I nodded, agreeing.

"Not tough enough. I took it easy on you. So it's settled then… partner," she said, putting her hand out for me to shake.

Looking in her eyes and then at her hand, I smirked. "Partner." I shook her hand. "You sure you can handle this, Ivy?" Things could get crazy, complicated, or whatever you wanted to call it, but truth be told, I wouldn't have put her in this position if I thought she couldn't handle herself. She already knew a lot, but whatever she lacked, I'd be here to put her on game.

"Whatever you throw my way, Ty," she confidently spoke.

"We gon' see about that, shorty. Partners, huh? Yeah, okay." I grinned, and she did the same. "Strictly partners." She tried correcting me, and instead of replying, I simply started to undress her with my eyes as we continued to shake hands.

Things were just heating up.

*To be continued*

CPSIA information can be obtained
at www.ICGtesting.com
Printed in the USA
LVHW051957171220
674450LV00014B/1309